Sometimes

the

Soul

Sometimes
the
Soul

*Two Novellas
of Sicily*

Gioia Timpanelli

W. W. Norton & Company

New York • London

Photographs © Karl Blossfeldt/Artist Rights Society

For information about permission to reproduce
selections from this book, write to Permissions,
W. W. Norton & Company, Inc., 500 Fifth Avenue,
New York, NY 10110.

The text of this book is composed in Centaur
Desktop composition by Platinum Manuscript Services
Manufacturing by Quebecor Printing, Fairfield Inc.
Book design by Judith Stagnitto Abbate

Library of Congress Cataloging-in-Publication Data

Timpanelli, Gioia.
Sometimes the soul : two novellas of Sicily / Gioia Timpanelli.
p.   cm.
Contents: A knot of tears—Rusina, not quite in love.
ISBN 0-393-02744-9
I. Sicily (Italy)—social life and customs—Fiction.
I. Title.
PS3570.I463S65   1998
813' .54—DC2I   97-47586
                                                              CIP

W. W. Norton & Company, Inc., 500 Fifth Avenue,
New York, NY 10110
http://www.wwnorton.com

W. W. Norton and Company Ltd, 10 Coptic Street,
London WC1A 1PU

2 3 4 5 6 7 8 9 0

to my mother and father,
Lena Romeo and Charles Timpanelli,
with love and gratitude

Sometimes the soul is tested. The body feels sore, the mouth dumb, the big red hands hang useless on their arms. Time passes. Surely, the soul will have its way. It lolls. Time passes. And the soul waits. Nothing happens. Come on, *make* something happen. Make lists! There are always urgent things to do, things to do for this morning, for today, for next week, for a month, for an entire year. But then a laziness takes hold, and nothing on the lists proves as urgent as this lethargy, so the lists are left out in the sun in a shopping bag, become bleached, illegible, are rained on, and finally forgotten under the beach chair. (No, not lists, certainly not lists. Poor, dear, little papers. It's too heavy a burden for them.) Minutes pass, hours, maybe a year, possibly a decade. At last, the soul is refreshed in the sweet company it has made.

Then, one day, it gets up and stretches. Today is not like yesterday. The soul notes the difference. To the neighbors, opening and slamming shut their doors, nothing seems to have happened. Nothing at all. Finally, now, the soul lifts its arms and with its graceful hands brings down the fertile rain.

A Knot of Tears

Sunday

Palermo, at the turn of the century

It was not only the absence of light in the room that was disturbing but also the windows themselves seemed to be closing in. No, "closing in" is not right, for it hints at light dimming, taking time like dusk to night, rather than the sudden and unnatural darkness that had now filled the house for months. When was it that all the windows and doors had been shut, bolted, secured for the long night? Just now, when a door opened a figure could be seen in the afternoon sunlight; and then when the door closed the figure with all the objects in the room was suddenly plunged into the unseen world.

Inside the Green Palace

B y chance the lamp went out. The woman standing in absolute darkness moved about unsteadily, groping for something familiar, but having turned herself around she could find neither the door to the garden nor the table which she knew stood solidly in the center of the room. From nowhere a gust of panic came and went. Finally, her arm hit the table's edge; she pulled out a chair, and since she was one of those people given to inadvertent sighing, sighed as she sat down. In this closed darkness nothing was reflected, nothing from within or from without for that matter: neither a glint from a spoon nor a line of moonlight. Then suddenly she felt an overwhelming oppression and an unfamiliar knot of tears welled up in her chest. She was surprised and tried to ignore it by saying aloud a line of poetry she had been reading in the study, something about the wind passing over a field of wheat, but she said instead, *"Un gruppu di chiantu,"* a knot of tears.

Now she felt confusion and the need of air, the need of air. She was a reasonable and moderate person, surely she could get hold of this, but instead she filled the room with a great sigh and said aloud again, *"Un gruppu di chiantu."* It prevented her from breathing easily. It would not be ignored. From where did this tight knot, entangled rope of tears come? She feared if she touched it, it would unravel her.

A light came from down a great hallway, and the housekeeper, an older woman with beautiful, serene eyes, entered, carrying a rather large lamp whose oblique rays played unsteadily with the iron bars of a topmost shutter. She put the heavy lamp down and looked at the young woman sitting so still at the table.

"Are you all right, *Signura?*"

"I feel suffocated, Agata. Suffocated."

The older woman turned toward her, sat down quietly beside her, and took her hand. Suffocated? Suffocated? It was a miracle that the young woman hadn't become ill before this. It was no wonder. This behavior was odd from the beginning. But she had not known the lady or her circumstances before coming to work as a housekeeper and the lady was *simpatica*, kind, gracious, human, and very, very sad. The two of them living inside a closed house! Imagine locking all the windows and doors and sitting for days, weeks, months, inside a cage of your own making! She had not been given a good enough reason for this strange arrangement, except that the lady desired to be alone, and that, of course, was the strangest reason of all.

"Ah! Signura Costanza," replied the housekeeper, "all things have a solution, or at least most things," she said with typical Sicilian reasoning. "Let's carry this table to the high window and open it so that you can see the busy life out on the *Corso* and get a change of air."

The table, heavier than the lady imagined and lighter than the housekeeper had feared, was finally perfectly placed. Costanza climbed up and with closed eyes breathed her first deep breath.

"Ah! Thank you, God!" (*Ah! Signuri vi ringraziu!*) And as that inadvertent "Ah!" left her lips, two men, sitting at a lawyer's bench just across the way, by chance heard that freeing word, looked up, and saw the blissful face of a beautiful woman in ecstasy.

"Oh! My God, look at that beautiful woman," said one of the men, a gentleman who was sitting with his lawyer. "Who is she?"

"I don't know," said the other man, giving her a closer look.

When Costanza saw the two men looking up at her with such interest, she withdrew slightly annoyed.

"But she's your neighbor. Haven't you seen her before?" asked the gentleman.

"It's strange but I haven't ever seen her. As a matter of fact, that palace has been closed for years. I didn't know anyone was living there now. Look at it—it still looks closed!"

"Who owns it?"

"I've heard a Neapolitan prince who never comes to Palermo, not since his mother died."

"I would like to meet that beautiful woman."

"*Cavaleri*, you and I both," answered the lawyer, still looking up at the open window. "Is she an apparition?"

"She is real," said the gentleman softly, "and she has taken my breath away. I must find a way to be introduced to her. My cousin Filomena must know her. Sooner or later everyone comes to her Thursday literary salon," he said confidently.

"Her strong face with those wide gray eyes and thick black braids reminds me of that painting of Titian's your uncle left you. The one they think is Minerva."

"Ah! But, my dear man, you are mistaken—this lady has brilliant violet eyes and is not as calm as Minerva."

The lawyer, suffering from impetuosity as well as envy, jumped quickly: "Whoever she is I will meet her before this week is up. And I will bet you a substantial amount that *I* will speak to her before you."

"It's a bet!" said the gentleman, putting his hand half in, half out, of his pocket. And tilting his head as if to say, "We'll see," he soon left the lawyer's in a better mood than when he had arrived. What had been asleep in him was now awake.

And so a number of lives moved toward Dame Fortune's table that night and with secret whispers left offerings there. Was it a chance gust of wind or the force of human wills? Coming from different directions, chance and will embraced like old friends, then arm in arm walked down the street together. "What is lost, will be found; what is hidden, will be revealed," said one.

"Don't be so sure, Friend. Maybe it will, maybe it won't," said the other.

Sometime on Sunday afternoon, between the midday meal and evening *passeggiata*, when time seems suspended and not a soul walked the streets of Palermo, a boy—a sailor by the looks of him—was strolling down the empty streets with a beautiful bright green parrot on his shoulder. The young sailor, who had a thin, birdlike nose on a handsome face, was whistling softly, with no movement from his lips, exhaling the perfectly tuned aria without any noticeable gesture. The parrot was singing and accompanying him loudly when an object was hurled onto the street from above, almost hitting the parrot and just nicking the boy on his finger. This action in turn loosened the finger's grip on a string tied to the parrot's leg, which immediately gave the bird freedom to fly up to the sill of an open window. (Someone looking carefully could have seen the boy, stretching forward up to the bird, lift slightly off the pavement with the bird's flight.) Seeing his companion hopelessly out of reach, the young sailor began talking to it. First, he was stern; next, he cajoled and begged; then finally, he commanded the bird to come to him at once. But the parrot, after cocking an eye down, turned its head and, ignoring him completely, disappeared through the open window.

The lawyer, watching all this, saw his chance and quickly crossed the street. "Young man, I see you are in a predicament. The lady who lives in that house won't easily open the door to you. I learned only this morning that she has closed the doors and never goes out and never lets anyone in. Let me suggest something that will help the both of us," he said, leading the young sailor to his office.

At the same moment from inside the Green Palace, the housekeeper saw the parrot alight. "Oh! *Signura*, look at that lovely bird." She climbed up on the table and offered her arm; the parrot walked from the window sash right onto it and like a drunken sailor on a plank bobbed back and forth on one foot to the next until it came down to a solid chair.

"A story! A story!" the parrot sang out and then continued whistling the aria it had been singing just seconds before. The women were delighted with the talking bird. Whose bird can it be? they asked again and again. From where did it come? A neighbor's? When Agata climbed up to the window to look out, the street was quite empty. "No one is here," she said. "No one at all."

"We'll get you a silver cage," promised Costanza.

"Pretty bird, come," she said, a deep rose madder coloring her cheek. The parrot cocked its head, looked down its nose at her, and almost smiled. "Mother, Mother, Beautiful Mother," it said. (*Mamma, Mamma, Bedda Matri.*) The women laughed. The parrot began a series of gurgling sounds deep in its throat, which Costanza imitated. It stopped, turned its head way round, listened for a few seconds, then moved quickly toward the answering voice. Now it imitated her voice and spoke back. A conversation had begun. The parrot was pleased, spread its green tail. The glimpse of color was startling. Again it spread its tail: now between the bright green feathers shone five bright yellow ovals. "Oh! How beautiful," she said, shuddering.

The parrot flew to the top of a golden mirror, walking back and forth, placing its feet carefully. Its eyes were shining. "A story, a story," answered the parrot.

"Tell us a story, come on," urged Agata.

"Find the cage, Agata, that great big one. Be sure it's the large silver one," she said as an afterthought.

"Oh, yes, yes, the silver one, but to tell you the truth, *Signura*, cages are cages."

"But this one is beautiful, the silver quite special."

Agata went off mumbling to herself, "Beautiful? When

are they beautiful? Ask those who are caught and put in them whether they see gold, silver, bamboo, or walls."

Agata remembered once when she was ten walking through a field of flax and coming upon a small wooden cage crowded with wild birds. They had been trapped and were now about to be sold for a mouthful, a miserable little mouthful. It was a terrible, terrible sight: the birds so close to the grass beat their fragile wings and threw their bodies against the bars, frantic to get out. Without even hesitating, she had pushed up the door latch with a single gesture and released them. "How did the birds get out?" everyone asked again and again.

"However," she said aloud coming into the kitchen, "this parrot was born in captivity or it would not be able to speak like us." She heard talking in what sounded like a human voice: "Once upon a time" (*Si cunta e si ricunta*), began the parrot again as if it were going to begin a story. (*Si cunta e si ricunta. Si cunta e si ricunta.*) "It is told and retold," it said again and again.

"Yes, go on, go on," coaxed Costanza (perhaps it had learned a little story), but the parrot was hanging upside down on the mirror to look at its image in the glass. It pecked lightly and looked up only when she repeated the early throaty sounds it had taught her. "Beautiful Mother, Beautiful Mother," it sang out in its clear and almost human voice. Then it began singing a familiar song. It was from a Sicilian opera. Was it from Bellini? she wondered. Oh! Yes, of course, it was from *La Sonnambula*. And then in a whisper the parrot began to say brokenly, almost inaudibly:

———

Ah! per me non v'ha conforto.
No; il mio cor per sempre è morto
alla gioia ed all'amor
Ah! per me non v'ha conforto.

Ah! for me there is no peace.
No; my heart is forever dead
to joy and love
Ah! for me there is no peace.

Costanza sang a bit of it with the bird—"Ah! for me there is no peace"—and for the first time in a long while she laughed at herself. And as she sang the words the parrot whistled, all the while moving about the mirror.

When Agata placed the silver cage on a huge empty sideboard off the large kitchen, the parrot flew to the top of it and, since the door was open, swung itself in, in one easy bird motion. She then put a handful of seeds into a fluted cup and water into a Venus shell which sat on an opposite ledge. The parrot bobbed its head up and down, chose a seed, split and ate it, then hopped to the open door of the cage, cooing and whistling the aria. It went to the little silver pool, extended its yellow neck, delicately dipped its beak, and drank the clear water.

Then suddenly there was a knocking at the front door. This knock sounded loud, echoing through the long, dark hallway. The striker, shaped like a roaring lion, now hit the door nail again. But the third knock was tentative. By the fourth knock, the hand let go of the lion's head so gently that the feeble tap it made did not reach the women's ears; only the parrot moved. And then, silence.

"Shall I go to see who it is?" asked the housekeeper.

"Too bad! It's probably the parrot's owner," said the younger woman.

Agata came back from the door out of breath saying, "There's not a living soul at our door, *Signura*. I wonder why they've changed their mind."

So by the time the streets had filled with people and then emptied again, water and all comfort given the new guest, a large brocaded silk with a raised golden image of The Judgment of Paris thrown over the cage, night descended equally on all the household.

Agata brought a lamp to her room, opened her small window, and breathed in the night air. (She did not think it was full of evil vapors, contrary to popular belief.) She watched the last running feet . . . going here and there, she thought . . . going here and there, wearing out their sad and sorry shoes and to what end? Where are they all hurrying to, where?

And the *Signura*, poor creature, what good could come from never seeing people? Never going out for a little walk, a *passeggiata*? The poor thing had turned their lives inside out by this strange behavior. Whatever this game was, it had gone too far. What benefit could come from being without good company?

But it was none of her business. And, of course, the old saying "It is better to be alone than badly paired" was right. Her poor mother had often repeated that to her, for solace surely, but Agata had not had the heart to tell her

mother that she enjoyed being a spinster, not compromis-
ing her sovereignty in her own home. Of course, she understood if the lady wanted to be unattached, but to live in a
closed house—that was too strange really. But then there
was her own life to think about.

"I am blessed with you," said her mother, "but when
I'm gone and you will be by yourself I worry. I can't imagine you alone in the house. Maybe your cousin's children
can come. A little company would be good." Her dear
mother. When would she ever get home? She missed the
children too. Everyone knows that without the company of
something real we are all lost. There was not even a cat in
the house. Then she thought of the beautiful parrot.

Thank you, God, for closing one door and opening
another, she prayed—a bit too literally?

The house was quiet, took on a breathing of its own now.
Costanza returned to the small study with its comfortable
settee and chair, covered in that deep wine and rust brown
velvet, dark vines and opened grape leaves hiding and
climbing in and out of the nap. She took down a small volume from the bookshelves which covered the walls,
arranged herself comfortably before opening the book, but
found she could not concentrate. She closed her eyes
instead and rested her head back upon the dark velvet
which framed her face. Nothing of the day's agitation
showed, for her heart was calm. It was here, in this room,
that she breathed normally again.

When finally she opened her eyes, she began reading

and soon was writing, all the while talking softly to herself, occasionally reading aloud, sometimes humming an aria from Bellini. Most of the night she spent like this. But she was not so foolish as to think she could go on exactly as she had before. Until the suffocation she had felt today, this peace had been almost perfect. For months she had loved it.

Time heals all wounds, people said. While time changed them, something closer to grace ameliorated them, nothing healed them. Time simply made another channel for the water to course down. Now she felt that the pieces which would make up her life could not be found in the company of others. She who had lived such a busy life was sure of that. She had gone to be quiet for as long as it took to find this new life.

At the Green Palace she was a closed house, an egg resting patiently, a snail waiting for water, a safe cocoon. Her friend's family house, especially its quiet places, was as she had imagined it. The old gardens, the dark, cool house, the quiet study where some nights she worked until dawn.

Once while in the middle of some Sicilian Greek lines about the passion of the gods for humans she saw vividly the wild woodlands of the ancient days, the great beauty in fields of wild grain, wild grain that once grew from the earth without tending. Other times she might see a large migration of eagles flying overhead or travel to the luxuriant meadows of wildflowers outside of Enna, the fields of her ancestors where it was said that Ceres' daughter had been stolen:

Proserpina fell from the fields of Enna
Fields where purple convolvulus grow
Down to the folds of the dark
Underworld

She couldn't remember the next lines, but she did remember her own Aunt Agatuzza telling her about the convolvulus, commonly called bindweeds, bindweeds which were always full of cocoons. "Let them be, child, and you will come back to a field of butterflies."

Then the pictures would be gone, and she would stare blankly for long minutes at a time. No matter how many things she read or wrote or remembered they all ended with a feeling of sadness. Only the garden was always marvelous. No one had cared for it for a very long time, and it had gone back to seed and wildflowers. Its beauty was in a subtlety only careful watching could perceive. She would sit in the sunny garden or the dark study for long hours each day, expecting something to arrive. It was as though she was waiting for some whisper from God. She had waited and waited, and then without warning it had finally come but it was not as soft as a whisper. It was from the painful knot of tears, the *gruppu di chiantu*, that this entire part of her life would find its meaning.

After months of absolute silence and abstinence, she had felt suffocated, she had needed some air, and the world had provided everything in a show of unexpected variety. Who would have thought so much could come in through one small window?

Monday

At the lawyer's

Early Monday morning the lawyer was at his bench watching for the sailor to return to the lady's house, ostensibly to get his parrot back, enchant his way in (what innocent airs the young fellow had!), and inform the lawyer by a signal the moment the lady left the house—and it had all been arranged in a ten-minute talk. Lady Luck had been with him, and he was on the way to winning both the bet and the beautiful woman. He almost felt happy.

When had he ever lost a woman or a bet? He always knew the score, the players, the prize. For this bet he knew his assets to the penny: intelligence, cunning, and a pleasing figure combined with an exceptional ability to show genuine interest in women, all women. This ability moved some of them toward him, often to their disadvantage. He needed these women who wanted his genuine attentions, however short-lived, for they gave back in great proportion to his investment. With the exception of a few troublesome entanglements, he came out of these encounters satisfied, and he felt he could not fail with this woman, for why should she be any different from the others?

God knows what his fool of a friend was cooking up, something pathetic and ineffectual no doubt. Every time he thought of his "friend" he grew angry. Why should "these people" have so much advantage? To hell with them! He knew how to help himself.

His family had lost everything in the war, and while this left his sisters and brothers cautious, it brought him a deliberate meanness, tempered with an impulsive generosi-ty, so that this morning he looked closely at the ragged boy who had been working hard for hours.

"Come here, kid, what's your name?"

"Tridicinu, sir."

"Here, Tridicinu, take this little extra for your work and come back on Saturday." The ragged child opened his calloused hands and accepted the gift with an elegance attributed usually to adults.

Without looking at his palm, the boy bowed and said, "Yes, sir. Yes, sir. I'll come for sure." He would put the extra two coins in his mother's pocket, without his brothers noticing, for they would be jealous of his luck, his usual little, little luck. These coins were good. He might even bring home a handful of dried chickpeas for her.

At the last moment the lawyer called the boy back. "Take this. It's for you, you alone. Buy yourself a sweet," he said, walking away, but then an impulse made him turn. In this moment of abandon the lawyer looked beautiful as the longer locks in the back of his head swung gracefully over his eyes, watching as the boy, unconscious of the man looking at him, picked up the heavy shovel and left whistling.

In his family, the lawyer's ability to rise in any situation, including social, was legendary. Where others of his class and occupation might have been consulted but socially ignored, or at best tolerated, he was welcomed. He was clever but showed it only for his rich and noble friends' advantage; he was ingratiating but never obsequious; he was decisive, balancing their languid and lazy habits; he got things done and they often didn't inquire how. What they never saw was his meanness, which did not bode well for gentle creatures who often depend on the natural fairness of others. Yes, these did poorly with him, for if he was in a bad temper, he would be brutal in his advantage over them. The old poverty had created a barrier in his feelings, so when he desired something, he would do anything to get it no matter what it cost others. He wanted the woman and the money with equal passion, and since he was always secretly angry, he was especially dangerous. It was only the memory of his childhood which privately animated him for there was no real eros in him, not even in his lovemaking.

Yet he was amusing himself in the gardens of Eros, a dangerous place for a man playing his own game; but he was daring and all his good luck gave him a cynic's sense of power. Privately, he laughed at his rich friend, so casual about his own real interests. He had so many rules which amused the lawyer. Codes of behavior, ideas about what was proper, permissible, and what was not. The lawyer believed that this foolishness sometimes stopped his friend from having the advantage over a situation, but then, because of the baron's wealth and position, he *did* have the advantage. He had no need to create it. This last thought, together with the fact that the sailor had not yet come back to the Green Palace, left the lawyer in a somber mood.

He suddenly felt weak all over and, remembering that he had had nothing to eat all morning, poured himself marsala, and just as he was about to drop the raw egg into the wine, he changed his mind, put down the glass, and holding the perfect egg between his fingers, took a needle, made two tiny holes in the smooth shell, put it to his mouth, and with great pleasure sucked its contents out. But when this was done, just before he shouted for his men to come in, the terrible but usual feeling of emptiness came over him.

At the gentleman's

The gentleman's house was full of ghosts, not the frightening spectral sort, but the kind that live in the lively objects ancestors leave behind. They had eaten at this table from China, drunk càlamo from that set of ancient Egyptian glasses while appreciating a fourteenth-century

French tapestry, handled the two-thousand-five-hundred-year-old Sicilian goddesses that had been unearthed from their country lands, and sat in front of this famous Venetian painting. Now *there* was a story: this Venetian scene had been one of four painted panels that had graced a Palladian villa; its three mates hung now in an English castle and had been there since the gentleman's ancestor, an Uncle Tiberio, had been unlucky at cards one cold, rainy month in Paris. This uncle lost his paintings through a kind of parsimonious temerity while playing Ambigu. At the moment he should have called for another card he kept an imposing king of diamonds, and the card that would have fallen to him went on to the fellow to his right, costing him the game and the third painting. He feared this luck might run in fours, and so he never gambled such high stakes again. Instead, he now began to frequent other places on rainy days, places which, although they did not cost him the loss of masterpieces, did nothing for the weight of his soul. Well, no mind, by the time he met his Maker he had almost forgotten that month in Paris and even now at the hands of a Flemish portrait painter looked dignified and judicious in an ambassador's robe. Everything in his palazzo had a story, and many of these stories were not even embellished. That's all that was meant by ghosts. The objects themselves were so vivid that they overshadowed the gentleman's young and watered-down character. But could one blame the twelfth-century Sicilian mosaic of the young Christ in the *cappella*? More than one life had been changed by the look in His startling, compassionate eyes.

No, it was simply that the gentleman was "a washed fish" (*un pisciu lavatu*), a good and dutiful fellow but a washed fish nonetheless. He had not yet begun to live his own life (whatever that might be), but he had known for some time that he was ready, poised at the edge of the sea. This one look at the lady in the window had revealed some part of his life which had, until that moment, remained hidden. He saw in her someone who might understand this hidden part of himself. That this hidden or even undeveloped self be seen by the Beloved is often asked of love, a request which frequently ends in disaster.

Since seeing her at the window, the gentleman could neither sleep nor eat. The business of the money made him a bit uneasy (his father would not have approved; and, of course, his mother would have never even heard a whisper about it). Yet he wanted to be, no, he needed to be the first one to speak to the divine woman. Yes, "Divine Woman" is how he thought of her now. Something in her excited praise in him. As a middle child, he himself had never gotten much praise from anyone: he had felt neglected and this led him to a secretive yearning which looked to the world like indifference and lethargy. But this time, he promised himself, he would complete his task. Something in his soul had been stirred and he felt it. He felt it.

He had been bred to honor, the kind that gets one to assume duty easily: he must not become poor, unlucky, or in any way diminished compared to those who had gone before. It could be a heavy burden. But fortunately, he was not lazy and he could not forget the needs of all who got their daily bread from him as they had from his mother and father before him, for he had a sweet heart. It was his turn now to provide whatever was expected and to do it graciously. His sister had married an exceedingly tall and thin prince with a foreigner's view of Sicily, for his family had come as legal advisors to conquerors some seven hundred years before. This sister had all she could do to keep her own languid group going in the ancestral palace near Cefalù.

And the youngest child was another problem. He studied classical Greek so intensely (beyond healthy knowledge, their father always complained) that he cared more about the writings of Diodorus Siculus and the possibility of discovering the actual cave of the Cyclops on the northeastern shore of the Island than he did about the grain harvest or the misery the countryside had just experienced. But to be fair to him, he himself ate little, lived in a fisherman's cottage at the sea, and gave what little money he had to an old couple who fed, clothed, and housed him as they did themselves. He had many literary friends. He published small articles in prestigious classical reviews that would not have dared insult him, of course, by paying for them.

The family ghosts whispered only to the middle child. This caused him to carry more of the family duty than was fair for one person. There was one thing about this that pleased him: with the exception of the single customary Easter visit of his sister, where amid long faces (*chi fungi!*) and emotional whispers the yearly accounting took place, he was accountable to no one. After Easter week she and her brood left, and he never saw them until the following year. His brother might turn up unexpectedly every three years or so—never at Easter. Well, he told himself, it's just as well. I work better alone.

Because he could not depend on his brother or sister he kept his own counsel, privately measuring himself only against his ancestors with words and sayings he had found in Latin poems that had moved him as a young man— Horace's "Ode to Simplicity," "Endurance," and "Fidelity to One's Trust," and many more—poems he now thought of frequently as he questioned his own life. Yes, all at once he felt something he recognized. That beautiful strong face, the ecstasy of her sigh, he recognized it. Was it from the poems? From his own dreams?

Now this bet was a bit of imaginative work. This bet! It pleased him to engage in it, and he did so with real enthusiasm. He continued his monthly duties—whoever worked or had worked for the family was fed, housed, and clothed—but listlessly. This lady in the window was his cordial—she warmed his cautious heart. About matters of the heart, he knew little, had never before this been willing to take a chance, something he now saw love required. The Beautiful One had kissed him into life, but if he was going to succeed he needed to do something. That afternoon at his cousin Filomena's, over a two-handed game of patience, he confessed his plight, and she introduced him to an actress.

For the promise of a good part and a bit of money, the actress wrote a scenario. How could the lady be enticed out of the house? Simple! She must leave the house to go to church. The actress would prepare a basket of out-of-season fruits and dressed as a genteel old "auntie" go to the door, present the basket, and talk the lady into going with her to a neighborhood church where the gentleman would be waiting.

Although he thought performers next to jugglers and pickpockets, he had been told that his ally was a good woman who had lived a long time in Paris and performed French classical theater. And it was at the moment she began speaking French to him that he became almost convinced her plan might work. He was eager to set it in motion and felt almost elated now as he waited for her in his family's sitting room, where he rarely admitted guests. It was in this place that he felt most comfortable. These ghosts were his; they spoke comforting words in his ear. And some had even been in love.

The vivacious woman who was shown into the room was impressed with the palace and the old family name, and it made her task seem justified, although she could not have said why. She had no reason to question her actions, which were bland enough in any case. What was this all about? A foolish woman closets herself in a large house and luckily catches the eye of this awkward gentleman who has family money, is well connected, and, although not altogether handsome, is well mannered—perhaps the only reliable trait in a man, the actress smirked to herself with a cynicism she never allowed anyone to see.

"I am so pleased you have come to help me in this," he said.

"Oh, yes, certainly. I don't see it as a difficult task," she answered, smiling at him.

"Oh, good, good." He hadn't noticed before that she had such long thick lashes and such bright blue eyes. "I have provided here all that you might need," he said.

"Oh, yes, sir. I am prepared to speak with this poor girl . . ."

But before she could finish, the gentleman waved her over to the delicate marble fireplace. Uncertain about his intentions, she went there thinking wildly, Does he want me to warm myself by a fire on this warm day? She knew that his class might be eccentric and went to the mantel with a strange smile on her pursed lips. He began waving his hand and pantomiming with his eyes and a nod of his head his intention for her to pick up the sealed envelope which he had carefully placed on the mantel next to the French figurine of a shepherdess. Is he mad? she wondered, as she saw his head and eyes moving wildly.

Finally she spied the envelope. "Oh, the money is here! That's what you mean," she said simply, picking up the heavy packet. He winced. (Perhaps no good can come from this, after all, he thought.)

They quickly arranged that she would try to coax the lady out of her house and to the church of San Calogero, where he would be waiting. "On the church steps," she said. "What could be more romantic? My costume is ready and the basket of out-of-season fruits is being assembled as we speak. So Wednesday morning," she said, "on the church steps. What could be more romantic, dear Baron? The rest will be up to the two of you." She laughed. He winced again. "You understand, sir," she just couldn't stop herself from saying, "I am only coaxing her outdoors and not necessarily into anyone's arms."

He winced again. "There is no question of that, madame."

"I thought not. Ah! those marvelous first words when one is in love . . ."

"Thank you, thank you," he said as he quickly walked with her to the door and rang for the butler, who immediately showed her out.

As soon as she was gone, he sighed loudly, poured himself some càlamo, the sweet wine his majordomo made each year at Christmas. This was the last bottle for a while. It was so sweet. He took courage and raised the perfectly colored wine in a toast to his dear gambling Uncle Tiberio, who smiled down on him benevolently—or was that mockingly?

Tuesday

By four in the morning, everyone was asleep in the Green Palace. The house itself seemed to sleep in a muffled and constant snoring, for no room was without the tiny sound or small creakings that happen to all sleepers, even this ancient house with its thick walls and crenellated head.

At five, the bird in the cage stirred and began moving about; then it squawked. At six, the bird squawked again. It seemed to be talking under the heavy cloth, a thing unusual for a parrot in a covered cage. At 6:10, Agata entered the dark kitchen with her lamp, uncovered the cage and opened its door, then turned to the kitchen and started the process of making coffee, then went to the turnstile door and unlocked it so that at 6:20 she could answer the knock, place a few coins on the ledge, turn the opening to face the street where the coins would be placed safely in a big leather purse and a small tin of fresh goat's milk could be placed on the ledge. The stile would be turned back, and the exchange satisfactorily completed, goat and man would go down the street, leaving her without a word of exchange or a bit of news.

At eight she went to listen at the study door. Costanza was moving about. She knocked, then went in with a wonderful healing bowl of bread soaking under hot milk and coffee. "For you!" said Agata. Costanza received the treasure and sat down dutifully to drink while she read.

At ten or thereabouts Costanza went into the kitchen to make some coffee and slice some bread and meat and see what Agata and the parrot were up to. As soon as she entered the kitchen, the parrot began talking to her: "*Bedda Matri,* let me tell you a story." It whistled and cooed, and Costanza sang and talked back as she began to boil water. She sang, "Ah! The heart is everything" (*Ah! tutto e il core!*), but the parrot did not join her. "Take this—the ring I'm giving you . . ." was one of the arias it usually sang, but it was quiet. She looked up. It was perfectly still, listening intently to something that she could not hear. It called, "Edmundo, Edmundo, where are you? Where aaa . . . re you?" The parrot swung to the top of the cage and listened again. It moved its head way around, adjusted its feathers and waited.

She listened, heard nothing, but was sure that someone was on the other side of the kitchen door. She went to it. Yes, she felt someone was there. Without thinking about it, she quietly unlatched a small shutter which covered a narrow, screened window, the kind seen in cloisters. She accomplished this easily without a sound. When she looked she saw the most guileless beauty she had ever seen. She saw the dark olive face, from the blue-gray Sicilian eyes, with their dark lashes, separate and thick, to the curve of a full upper lip and no more. The expression in the soft eyes was compassionate and still. It did not look back or see her; it asked nothing for itself, not even recognition. It was like seeing a beautiful, small portrait in which the eyes looked deeply at the world, without being aware of a painter or onlooker. It was as though he was waiting for an exchange from another world. This single fact affected her. She stood mesmerized for a few seconds until the stranger turned and broke the spell. He went off a few steps to look up (obviously debating with himself about knocking), and now she saw that at the curb was a young sailor. "Oh, yes, the parrot's owner," she sighed.

The sailor went back to the door. Costanza moved away from the peephole, and when the bell finally sounded in the kitchen she had walked around the large marble table at least twice. She sat down and waited. The bell rang gently again. Slightly agitated, she went to the heavy door, unbolted the lock with difficulty, and for the first time in months she opened the door and stood facing him.

"Good day, *Signura,*" he said with a short bow, his voice full of courtesy. "Did a parrot fly in through that window yesterday?"

"Yes," she answered, looking toward the great silver cage. The parrot stood perfectly still looking at them. Then it turned its head and listened.

"Nello," called the sailor, "what are you doing here,

bothering this lady? Forgive us, *Signura*, for the intrusion," he said, bowing again. "Come, Nello, you belong on a ship with rowdy seamen, not in a lady's house. Come down. Come, Nello, they're waiting for us in Mondello. Come, be reasonable."

"Do you always reason with parrots?" asked Costanza, amused. The parrot, looking dignified and indifferent, stayed as far away from the young man as possible.

"Yes, I try, because birds reason better than most people."

"That's true enough," said Costanza, smiling, as the parrot flew to the young man, causing a great stir of feathers and confusion in the kitchen. The parrot settled on his friend's shoulder and began stroking his cheek. The sailor bobbed his head up and down, giving the strokes back.

"I see," said Costanza, "that the parrot has taught you parrot reason. Or is that filial love?" she said teasingly.

"A little bit of both, probably," he answered seriously.

For a brief second the young sailor looked up at the lady without looking into her eyes impolitely and said, "My name is Edmundo Patanè," and then bowing slightly he added, "I'm from Sciacca."

"I know a Patanè family from Sciacca. I went to school with the youngest daughter."

"You must mean Rosaria. Our families live near each other," he said.

And before he could apologize a second time for the intrusion (strangers do not easily go in and out of Sicilian homes), Agata came into the kitchen saying, "Oh! Too bad! The parrot's owner is found. So, you're a sailor with this

lad, eh? Good day," she said. "Good day," he answered, low-
ering his head. Names were given all around.

"The parrot's name is Nello," Edmundo said.

On hearing his name the parrot began saying: "Let me
tell you a story, *Mamma Bedda, u cuntu, u cuntu,* Edmundo,
Edmundo, where aa . . . aa . . . re you?" The last "where are
you?" was said in that singsong way used by children in
hide-and-seek games. This song had an amazing effect on
everyone. The whole atmosphere changed. "Where are
you? Where a . . . a . . . a . . . re . . . you?" the parrot sang
in the playfully intimidating song, the "are" rising to a
high pitch. "Here I come, ready or not. You can't hide from
me. I'm about to find you," he said. They all looked at the
parrot and laughed. The young man became self-conscious
for the first time. (He was remembering the words recently whispered in his ear.)

"I'm sorry, *Signura,* for the trouble we're giving you. Is
there something I can do before we leave? Maybe carry that
huge cage away?"

"No, no, thank you all the same. We've enjoyed having
Nello," said Costanza.

"Yes, by all means, yes. The nuisance is worth the
seeds," said Agata.

Now it looked as though bird and young man would
be gone in seconds. Agata opened the door. The young
man, with the parrot on his shoulder, had turned to go
when Agata, seeing him search his pockets, stepped toward
him saying, "Wait! You don't have the string that was
attached to his foot. I'll look for it." When the door closed,
a man across the street ran to the back room to call the

lawyer, who put down the contract he was reading to himself and smiled.

The sailor said, "Or perhaps, *Signurina*, you might find a stronger one."

While Agata went off in her not-so-fast running step, Costanza said, "Will you sit down? Will you take a late morning coffee with us? We were just going to make some."

"Oh, yes, gladly. Thank you," he answered, putting the parrot back in the silver cage, then sitting in the place she offered. And for the first time, the sailor looked up at the one window, through which the parrot had flown in from the street.

"You've taught your bird to sing opera," said Costanza, turning. "And you're an admirer of Bellini. A parrot who sings bel canto is remarkable."

"Yes, madame, you're right. I love Bellini's music. Nello heard me singing while I worked as cabin boy for the captain of the *Ulysses*. But now that I'm a seaman, we don't have the same time together."

Agata came back out of breath. "I can't find any cord good enough for this great escape artist, not even the original string that I remember seeing."

Some talk followed about never finding the right string at the right time, and they all sat down at the table. They drank the first cup, and Costanza poured the remainder, giving more to the guest and sharing what was left with her companion. Agata passed the sugar in a bowl on which bright yellow-and-green decoration had been painted, a design of benign and leafy dragons, an old pattern paint-

ed in the same way by different hands for four hundred
years or so. It was all so familiar somehow, like a family's
Sunday together. They, all three, felt a kinship. The pleasing silence was broken by Nello, who rang out, "Edmundo,
Edmundo, where a . . . a . . . a . . . rrre . . . you?"

The listeners at the table again had an immediate
response to the game's singsong. Without an exact memory
each felt united in the common experience. "Where a . . . a
. . . are you? I'm going to find you. Here I come, ready or
not." So when the young man rose reluctantly, saying, "I
guess it's time for us to go," all three felt truly bereft, as when
a friend was called home by parents before the game was
over.

And because of this feeling, it was agreed that
Edmundo would stay and help them put away the provisions in the storerooms. Now they all went to look at the
huge grain sacks. "Look! Something has been eating at the
sacks," said Costanza.

And what with this and that the morning soon passed.
At one o'clock Agata began preparing a simple meal. When
Costanza came into the kitchen, she found both the parrot
and his mate: the one, in and out of the garden, sorting
and carrying, while the other was happily walking in and
about his cage, whistling the aria from *La Sonnambula*, which
had become the household anthem. She had not felt so
happy in a kitchen in years. Everyone was pleased with
work.

So when Agata came into the kitchen and said,
"*Signura*, it's so near dinner. Should we invite the young
man to stay? Finish the work? What do you think, *Signura*,

is it a good idea or not?" Costanza answered, "It's a good idea, Agata. I know his family. It's as safe as asking a cousin."

And so, with much talk, the young man and parrot stayed for the midday dinner, then for the small evening meal. And when it was time to leave that night, Edmundo had not put all the sacks away ("This task needs 'the help of God,' " said Agata). So it was amiably agreed that he would stay a few days until the *Ulysses* sailed. In the meantime, he would tell them about the adventures he'd had at sea and put away the endless sacks and provisions some master chandler had made for this tossed ship. "But, my boy, are you sure you want to be in this stuffy old house?" Agata asked.

"Where else do I want to be? Getting in trouble with those rowdy sailors?" Edmundo responded, smiling. "Much better here than the usual few days in Mondello, when here I could be useful to you," he added graciously. An officer's field bed, found in the marvelous attic, was set up off the kitchen. Agata brought in an armful of heavy linens, and without much ado, the household settled down quite naturally to include the parrot and his companion.

And so, for a chance nick on a finger, more gifts were heaped upon Fortune's table that night. And the lawyer, who now believed he knew exactly what was going on in the closed fortress across the way, was satisfied. From his rooms that night, no one watched the palazzo's doors, and the cunning man had a passable night's sleep. The gentleman dreamed marvelous dreams about the sea and a beautiful woman walking toward him from the waves, but there was one troubling episode where Jupiter as Tonans, the Thunderer, showed anger and the sky opened. And at midnight, he was awakened by the lightning and thunder of a great storm passing over Palermo on its way into the interior.

Midnight and Costanza

The wind comes from the sea tonight. It roars outside and bangs even the closed shutters. It finds the rigid places and loosens them. Not stopping for a moment, it attacks the fortress in all its weak places. Running now through the walled garden, it tosses the palm trees, bending the old ones in the direction of their already stormy history. Two cats stop in their pursuit, crouch down inside a broken column base. Their prey, momentarily distracted, lifts its large pointed nose, smells the strong salt air, then hurries on to a hole where its young are waiting.

This strong wind awakens the parrot Nello, who shifts about his cage and murmurs, "Okay, okay, okay, captain" (*Va bene, va bene, va bene, capitano*); the wind moves the sleeping Edmundo, who turns and whispers a name into the crook of his arm; it gets Agata up to secure the latch at her window and stuff a large piece of linen into a pernicious crack. She picks up the small image of the Blessed Mother from the tiny bedstand, puts it to her lips and begins to say her prayers, all the while snuggling back

down into the warm sack her body makes with her old
quilt. Finally, at the last *"Ave Maria, gratia plena . . ."* (Hail,
Mary, full of grace . . .), she falls into the sound her mind
makes, *"benedicta tu in mulleribus . . ."* (blessed art thou among
women . . .), and at the last words falls asleep, just as a light
goes out in the lawyer's office across the way.

Now, only a colony of nocturnal insects, sundry mice,
and the woman writing at her small desk are awake inside
the Green Palace. Costanza writes in her diary:

> *Tonight I am traveling between worlds. The great mountains and
> caves below the sea are alive with the tiniest of creatures. A school
> of golden fish swim alongside of me for a long while and then sud-
> denly turn off, and I see coming toward me a huge fish, its open
> mouth gathering infinitesimal food with slow, systematic calm.
> Now I turn and swim from this deep crevice to the top of a coral
> reef, just missing the colony of spikey urchins, and then up, up, up.
> The ecstasy of this moment, having left one place and not yet hav-
> ing arrived in the other.*
>
> > *But as soon as I write this I am frightened. In the past
> ecstasy has brought danger. Am I now a small and timid crea-
> ture, whisker-twitching through my life? Yet for me when ecsta-
> sy has been coupled with too much action, like poor Icarus I am
> in danger of forgetting consequences, feeling the power of ecsta-
> sy, forgetting the power of grace. One of my childhood friends,
> with his wild ways and gentle heart, is now forced to sit day
> after day in a decrepit office filling his life with empty papers
> and faulty pens. What lack of grace brought him to a desert of
> pain so far from home? When we children swam in the warm*

sea we could not have imagined that spirit could sit in dusty places.

Instructions on measurement or lessons on metaphor were not what Icarus needed from his father on that bright sunny day.

I take consolation tonight in remembering. Although I know we humans at times have short, selective memories, our internal gods do not. They forget nothing. While we are asleep or awake, these little gods chatter intimate stories to anyone who will listen, and we get away with nothing, neither in exile nor in isolation. We cannot help but betray ourselves. Tonight when I heard a string plucked, the sound continued as the trembling of joy in my body, and I remembered everything and yearned again. But like Daedalus, I too, am afraid tonight. Between the soul and my self there is some distance.

Wednesday

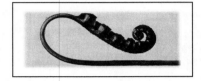

A bird was found with a broken wing
Because it thought a human thing
was the sky

The street in front of the Green Palace was crowded; the markets in midmorning did a brisk business. There were so many people hurrying about their own urgent affairs that the actress had to move slowly, carrying her precious basket of fruit carefully in her arms so as to spoil neither the fruit nor her equanimity, for without both she might as well go home. But she liked the gentleman and she liked a good game, and since she was still in that first moment of resolve, it carried her to the lady's front door, where she was greeted by a huge brass door knocker in the shape of a lion's stern face. With the lion's jaws in her hand, she knocked decisively and waited. (Two men at the lawyer's bench across the way stared at her, and then one disappeared into the dark caverns of the building.) She then tried the kitchen door, where she rang vigorously. The peephole was opened immediately by a frowning Agata. On taking in the looks of the older woman dressed in genteel gray silk, Agata asked, "What do you wish, *Signura*?"

"Hearing that the lady of the house is new to our church, I have come to say a few words of greeting," said the kindly looking woman, speaking too loudly. (Some people passing stopped to look at her.)

"Wait a moment, I will ask," Agata snorted.

"Who is she? Have you seen her before?" asked Costanza disinterestedly.

"Well, not exactly, but she looks familiar, like someone's kindly and well-meaning aunt. Yours perhaps?"

"Not mine."

At the open door, Costanza had not even said two words when she was surprised by the basket of incredible fruits. Once in, the woman lost no time in cajoling the younger woman into a pleasant and ordinary place. "My dear *Signora*, we have not seen you at mass. Are you not going? Come out, it is a good day, and we are in plenty of time." On a sudden impulse, Costanza rose, went to the large bureau, chose a shawl, and was about to walk out the door with the "auntie" when an extraordinary fuss began in the alcove. The parrot was standing on the cage pulling out his beautiful bright green feathers and shouting, "Mother, Beautiful Mother, hear my story. Hear my story." The bird now moved wildly around the cage, shouting and crying aloud.

"Oh, you poor thing," said Costanza. "Please stop pulling your feathers out."

But Nello screamed and cried all the more: "A story, a story, let me tell you a story."

Turning to the auntie, she said, "I'm sorry but there is a problem right now so I can't come out with you. Tomorrow, I will come with you to mass. Yes, tomorrow." Agata quickly opened the kitchen door and showed the actress out just as it began to rain lightly. (Across the way, the lawyer put his arm around the shoulders of his henchman, leaned down and said, "You see, nothing to worry about.")

When the door closed, Agata slipped the bolt, turned, and saw a laughing Costanza beside the parrot, soothing it with her talk and her clucking. "A story! A story!" the parrot called out just as Edmundo appeared from the garden wiping his earthy fingers. "Would you really like to hear a story?" he asked.

"Yes, yes, we've been trying to get one from Nello since he came," answered Costanza.

"I love the old stories," he said. And without any further ceremony, Costanza and Agata sat down at the kitchen table to hear Edmundo tell an old folktale he had heard from his great-grandmother.

The First Story

{ *Primu   cuntu   di   lu   pappagaddu* }

"*Si cunta e si ricunta,*" the parrot said.

"It is told and retold," began Edmundo with a proper Sicilian beginning. "There was a King, and this King had an only daughter who loved dolls, and of all

the dolls she had, she loved one best of all. It gave her
pure delight. This doll she dressed and undressed, put
to sleep—in short, did everything that one does for a
child. One day, the King wished to have a picnic in the
countryside, so the Princess, of course, brought her
beloved doll along with her. She played happily in the
woods for a long while, and when it was time to eat, she
joined the others at table. After they had eaten and all
had been cleared and put away, the King sent word that
she was to hurry along and join him immediately in the
royal carriage. So she ran to the coach, where he was
impatiently waiting for her. In this hurry what do you
suppose she forgot? Her precious doll. That evening,
just as she was about to enter her bedroom, she remembered her doll and, without thinking, turned in her
steps, went down the stairs, out the door, and into the
world to find her precious companion. But after a
while, she realized she was so lost that she could not
even find her way back home. She went from one town
to another, searching first in this place and then in
another, but she was so lost that no matter what she did
she could not find her way back to her family.

Finally, in her wanderings she found herself in
front of another royal palace, where she asked, "Who
is the sovereign of this place?"

"The King of Spain," the people said. So she
thought she would try her luck there. She entered the
great hall and begged to be taken in and given a place
to sleep. When the King saw her, he not only gave her
a place to stay but also treated her as his own daughter.
So the lost Princess found a home with the King of
Spain. In no time, she was at home in the palace. She
truly acted *La Patruna.* The King, you see, had no children

of his own about, and he did everything for her that a parent does for a child. He cared for her royally. And since she was *La Reginedda*, the Princess, he even gave her twelve royal ladies-in-waiting.

But, you know how it is, since Envy, the great equalizer, is everywhere (*la 'mmidia e 'nta li pari*), the Twelve Ladies-in-Waiting began to go against *La Reginedda*. "Look at her! Who knows who she really is? And where she comes from?" they said behind her back. "Who says she has to be our princess! This has to end now." So the next day they asked her, "Do you want to come visiting with us?"

"Yes, I would like to go with you, only, of course, if Father agrees," said the Princess.

"To get him to agree, do you know what you should say to him?" They slyly tell her, "Say 'On the soul of your daughter, will you let me go?' As soon as he hears these words, 'on the soul of your daughter,' he will quickly agree to your wishes. When he hears those words, he always consents," they lied.

And so the Princess did exactly as they said, but instead of being pleased when he heard "on the soul of your daughter," the King became so enraged that he shouted, "Leave my presence," and with that he opened a door she had never even seen before and pushed her through it, saying, "Good riddance."

She was in a maze of underground corridors, and after a long, long time she found a door. She opened it and found herself in a small room facing a golden birdcage with a mechanical golden bird sitting on a perch. And next to the cage, in the shadows, sitting on a narrow bed, was a pale young woman. "How can I help you?" asked the Princess. The young woman put

her finger to her lips, and *La Reginedda* understood that
she could not speak for there was the shadow of a tiny
lock fallen on her lips from the golden birdcage.
"How can I help you?" asked *La Reginedda* again. The
pale woman pointed to her pillow. The Princess went
to the bed, lifted the pillow, and found a small gold
key. The young girl pointed to the cage, and when the
Princess quickly opened the lock on the cage, the
shadow on the mouth opened as well, and the pale
young woman let out a long sigh and the golden bird
began to sing.

Now the poor thing told *La Reginedda* her story. "I
am the daughter of a king, but the magic lock prevents
me from speaking. A Magician and his Giant Servant
come at midnight and bring me a huge tray of food.
They unlock the cage, the little bird begins to sing, and
I can speak and eat. Then after I eat the bird stops
singing and the cage door is locked, the key goes under
the pillow, and everything is as it was before. They leave
and once again I cannot speak until the next day. This
happens every day. They, themselves, never speak a
word to me."

"Tell me," said *La Reginedda*, "how can I free you
from this terrible prison?"

"And how would I know! The only thing I can do
is ask the Magician when he comes. You hide under the
bed so you can hear us talk, and then you can think
about what you can do to help me."

"Good! good!" said the Princess.

They put everything back as it was: the key under
the pillow, *La Reginedda* went under the bed. With all
this talking it was almost midnight. At exactly the hour
when it is neither this day nor the next, there was an

awful sounding crash (*un gran fraccassu*). The earth trem-
bled. There was lightning, thunder, smoke, a terrible
odious smell. Lo and behold! the Magician appeared
followed by the Giant, who carried a large brass tray
with an enormous dinner in one hand, and in the other,
two torches to light the place. They opened the little
lock, and the golden bird began to sing, and the
enchanted woman said, "Magician, I just had a
thought. For curiosity's sake, what would it take for me
to leave this place?"

"You want to know a lot, my daughter," he
answered.

"Oh, let it go then. I don't want to hear it."

"But I *want* to tell you. First, it is necessary to prepare a ring of bonfires around the castle, between that
spot on the hill over there and the castle. Then exactly
at midnight when I am seen on that road, all at once the
bonfires must be lit, and as the fires are lit you will find
that I have disappeared, and you, yourself, will be completely free. This place will also be gone and you will be
home once again."

"Don't worry, your secret is safe with me. It's as if
you had said it to no one," said the young girl.

When the Magician and the Giant left, *La Reginedda*
came out from under the bed. "This is all very interesting. The only thing is that I will have to first get out
of this place, then arrange for the huge bonfires to be
prepared—and all before tomorrow midnight. I don't
have much time, but I will do it!" she said. After kissing her dear sister good-bye—you see, they already
called each other "sister"—she left.

The Princess walked and walked in those endless
corridors and finally began to call for help: *"Help! Help!"*

And again: "*Help! Help!* Whoever hears me, come and get me out of this place. *Help now!*" She even called, "Father, Father." The King heard her and sent his servants to show her the way out of the maze. The Princess told the King everything she had learned. The King, under the Princess' supervision, had all the bonfires prepared. When everything was ready, she said, "Coordinate your clocks, for this must happen exactly on time—at midnight."

When the Princess was sure everything was done exactly as she ordered, she went down again to be with her little sister. The Princess opens the lock on the golden cage, the bird begins to sing, the little shadow lock disappears, and the pale young woman and *La Reginedda* talk about their plan. "Courage," she said, looking at her watch. "It's time for me to light the fires and for them to come. Together we will win!" The sisters kissed each other good-bye.

Now the Princess knew her way out of the maze, and on the road exactly at midnight she lit the fires all around the castle. And with *crackle* here and *cracklecrickle* there, the fires began to burn. Everyone at the castle, up and down, here and there and all about, came out and all said, "Look up at the hill!" And finally the Magician and the Giant came over the hill walking toward the castle. They kept coming and the fires burned and they kept coming, but suddenly, before everyone's eyes, they disappeared, completely disappeared—Magician and Giant—as if they had never been. The Princess ran back to the young woman, and soon they were dancing and laughing. She was free. She could speak and laugh and sing, and in her hand was the golden cage and she opened the door and the mechanical bird became a beautiful golden bird that flew away singing its beautiful song.

When the King saw the two young women embracing and dancing, he said, "Ah! my daughters!" The young woman and the King embraced. "*Figlia mia, figlia mia,* my darling daughter, finally, you are free!" Then looking at the Princess he had adopted, he said, "I, myself, had no power over this magic and only through the bravery of a stranger could we be disenchanted. You have been sent to us. The misfortune you had of not finding your way back home has become our good fortune, and now it will become your fortune as well for I give you my gold crown." And saying this he took off his crown and held it toward the Princess.

"No, no, Your Majesty, thank you all the same. You can put your crown back on your head. I am already the daughter of a queen and king. I have a crown of my own."

May the birds continue to sing freely on their own and we too. And this story now over, the Princess embraced them both and they all lived happily together.

These events were told throughout the world, and the Princess' fame was known in many places. And you know how people are—for a while they spoke about nothing else. They talked about the great courage and generosity of the Princess who had liberated the pale woman she called "sister."

And they stayed happy and content,
And here we are without a cent.

And with one of the many old endings, Edmundo finished the story about the Princess and the young woman she freed.

————

After the story Nello jumped on the sailor's shoulder and caressed his friend's cheek. "So the parrot liked the story," said Agata, getting up to put the water on to boil.

"And I loved the story, Edmundo," said Costanza thoughtfully. There was no direct discussion of the tale that day, but the story with its humble words, simple events, and complex images affected all of them (a magical lock on a young woman's mouth, really terrible! thought Costanza; really true, felt Agata): Edmundo loved telling it, Agata loved hearing it, and Costanza had been moved by its implications. In a year of Good Fridays, a small resurrection of spirit was stirring. Well, as usual, the old tales had uncanny truths in them, and Costanza had often seen this princess rescuer in the everyday world, not a worldly princess but one of the heart. *La Reginedda*, thought Costanza, is in someone like Agata. What did it mean that *La Reginedda* could not find her way back home?

That afternoon when the rain had stopped, Costanza sat quietly in the garden next to the jasmine which climbed over the old stable's walls and was rewarded for her patience by seeing a lively bird, with its straight thin bill moving imperceptibly, systematically walk up the wall and then at the top fly away.

Midnight   in   the   study

Costanza wrote in her diary:

*The rain has stopped for the moment. A large rat carrying her sod-
den newborns in her mouth moves them one by one from the nest
down through a trapdoor while water from a gargoyle falls vio-
lently on the back of a steel gray cat. The hunched cat hopes he is
invisible under the trellis. He watches this running back and forth
out of half-closed eyes, pretending disinterest in this weighty problem, figuring his chances with the large and alert mother. A story
for an English naturalist to tell and draw, showing life's impar-
tiality so that the painful play of one of the world's hide-and-seek
lessons can be learned by young and old alike. And how would she
have it turn out? On the side of the mother rat? The cat must have
been very hungry to have even entertained that pounce; the rat had
fierce instinct on her side as well as a mob of friends and rela-
tives. In the end the cat did not act injudiciously, although he did
look foolish in all that rain licking his paws before he slipped away.*

*Sitting inside the palazzo, midmorning, a visit from a neigh-
bor with much rosette on her cheeks, inviting me to go to mass with
her. How did the ladies know I was here? Something is not quite
right about her, but what? Almost everything. But her visit was
good for it got Edmundo to tell an old story, and then because of
all this company and family spirit, Agata was in such a joyful
mood she sang old love songs all day.*

*I must write Alfonso tomorrow and ask him about the folk-
tale which Edmundo told. I have heard it before. I think it is
already in Giuseppe Pitrè's first collection, but I'm not sure; is
this a fragment of a longer story? What a series of powerful and
not-so-simple images. I still have not gotten over opening a door*

to find a pale woman who has a lock on her mouth. What inter-nal magic works on keeping her silent? And who are these two sis-ters, one silent and the other heroic? Edmundo was a good storyteller. Agata and I saw and felt the story as he told it. Telling is immediate and fleeting. The English naturalist writing the story of the rat and cat has other joys and problems. Writing and telling—they don't compare easily. Birds and stones.

Then closing her diary, Costanza went to the book-shelf and took down her notebook and under the heading "Moments of Fiction and Biographical Lies" wrote:

There once was a woman who loved freedom even more than she loved the sun and the moon. One day she could not find a key and immediately felt a desperate panic. After the key was found she laughed at her foolish worry, but within the hour, on not finding a book where she thought she had left it and feeling the very same fear, she began to observe these little momentary losses and her responses to them. Over the next few days she saw that each time she misplaced a number of small items—a pen, a brooch, the same key again—she felt a sudden fear which was totally out of pro-portion to the object temporarily lost. These wild traces she noted with increasing alarm, for there seemed to be no end to them.

One morning she awoke with that same panic and, since she was still half asleep, closed her eyes again and saw that she was in a cave, an underground kitchen, at the center of which was an ancient stone hearth, and deep inside the hearth was a great mound of ashes, apparently cold, but she could "see" that down in the cen-ter, completely hidden, was a glowing piece of burning coal which never went out, and suddenly she felt an overwhelming elation as though she had been shown something. When she awoke she was ecstatic and danced around her room until exhausted she fell upon the bed and rose with tears streaming down her quiet face. The

dream had brought her to a truth so real she could not ignore it.
That day she stayed in bed and did none of the running about for
the hundred social chores which made up her life. Everyone around
her went on as always but she had slipped away. She could not
ignore what she had seen. That night after dinner she did not go to
meet her friends for a coffee and literary talk but went instead to
her own study, sat down, and changed her life.

Costanza put down her pen and smiled. She had
remembered the beginning of the folktale: it was about a
woman who locked herself inside a house (she couldn't
remember why) and two men trying to get her out of the
house. What does the parrot have to do with it? Oh! of
course, the parrot tells the story that beguiles her to stay
inside the closed house, but she couldn't remember what
happened after that.

Thursday

A terrific surge of traffic came thundering down the *Corso*. People had to jump aside and one pushed the actress, who had already been startled by the noise, which was gone in seconds before the crowd adjusted itself again. By Jove, she thought, I'll take that as a sign from Jupiter, powerful charioteer and warrior, protector of Thursdays, powerful Thun-derer, or was that a different god? Oh! why did she begin certain and end a bit confused?

It was not yet eleven when the kindly looking "auntie" came again with another basket of rare fruits to the Palazzo Verde, rang the bell, and greeted Costanza with a question about the state of her soul.

"My soul?" said Costanza.

"It would be a good thing, *Signora*, to come with me to mass today as you said you would yesterday. I am quite worried about you; do forgive an old lady's concern," said the actress, moving the corners of her mouth up in a prissy smile.

"Yes, it's true that I said I would go with you to holy mass," said Costanza, getting up to get a wrap, when the parrot again started to screech, "*Traditore! Traditore!*" and wildly moved about the cage, feet over head, to end up upside-down crying, "A story, My Lady, a story!"

Costanza froze, looked at the parrot intently, turned back to the stranger, and sighing went to the door saying, "Thank you for coming again, but this is not a good time for me. Another time, no doubt, and I will be able to join you, certainly on Sunday." She opened the door, and the woman was out on the street as Edmundo began, "*Si cunta e si ricunta . . .*" (It is told and retold . . .)

The Second Story

{ *S e c u n n u   c u n t u   d i   l u   p a p p a g a d d u* }

And so, Signuri, it is told and retold, there was a king, and he had an only child, a daughter as beautiful as the sun and moon. When she became eighteen, a stranger asked to marry her. "What do I want with a stranger from far away? Who knows those towns and who wants to go there?" she said angrily. And she refused him with many disparaging words, many disparaging words. Little did they know that this stranger knew some terrible magic used for unrequited love.

A little time passed and she was overwhelmed by a serious illness. The great doctors could not diagnose this sickness. Her body went into torturous convulsions like a rope free of a sail. Her eyes rolled to the back of her head, and no one could get to the bottom of it. The poor father rang the great old council bell and called all the wise people of his little kingdom. When they had assembled, he told them the situation and ended by saying, "Honored ones, my dear daughter loses ground each day; nothing the doctors do is of any use; what do you think I should do?"

They answered, "Your Majesty, there is a young woman who saved the daughter of the King of Spain; find *her* and *La Reginedda* will tell you what is needed to save your daughter."

"So be it! This advice is propitious; I will do as you say." And so he ordered ships to be readied to sail and said, "If the King of Spain refuses to allow her to come, leave this glove as a token of battle, and if he still refuses, declare war!"

The ships sailed, and one morning they found themselves in the land of the King of Spain, where amid great pomp and ceremony the ambassador presented his papers with their request for *La Reginedda* to come back with them; when the King read the letter, tears came to his eyes. "I will be happy to fight you but you will never get this princess."

At that very moment, *La Reginedda* enters and seeing the King so upset asks, "What is the matter, Your Majesty?" She sees the letter and reads it. "So, what are you afraid of? I'll go to this king."

"What! You would leave us so easily?"

"I'll just go, see what is the matter with the young woman and then come back again." She embraces and kisses her sister good-bye, and leaves quickly.

Except for a few squalls and some major engine trouble, the sea journey was uneventful. When she

arrived at the King's palace, he hurried to greet her, saying as soon as he saw her, "If you free my daughter of
this illness, I will give you my crown!" (She laughs, saying to herself, "Look at this! There are two now talking about giving me their crowns!")

"Listen, Your Majesty, I have my *own* crown. Let's
see what's wrong and forget the crowns." When she saw
the young woman in such an awful state, she turned to
the King and said, "Get me good broth and some other
things of substance." Immediately they were prepared
and presented to her. "Now listen to me carefully. I am
going to close myself in with your daughter; and no
one must come in to disturb us, because at the end of
three days, she will come out of her room alive and well
or, God forbid it, not at all. Now listen to what I tell
you: in the meantime, even if *I* knock and tell you to
open *do not open the door*." Everything was ready; she
closed herself in with the sick Princess.

But once inside what does *La Reginedda* realize? Of
all things, she has forgotten to bring the light to ignite
the candles inside the dark and closed room. She goes
to the window, opens the shutters, and sees a fire burning brightly on a hill nearby. At the sill, she finds a silk
ladder and quickly climbs down and goes toward the
fire, carrying the candle to be lit. She sees that it is a
small fire under a kettle, and standing above it is a
stranger dressed in the clothes of some distant country.
"What are you doing, honored sir?" she asks. "My king
wants for to marry the princess of that palace there,
but she refuse and I sit here to do magic but nothing
work so I wait and wait and keep magic in pot boiling.
Soon she change mind."

"Oh! You poor fellow, you must be tired. Why
don't you take a nap for a while and I'll stir your pot?"

"Thank you, only I must ask to you not to disturb or take anything from here."

"No, don't worry, I understand," said the Princess. And he fell asleep immediately. The Princess, hearing his loud snores, with all her might turned the pot over and all its contents spilled out. She lit her candle from the burning fire and instantly everything melted: fire, stones, pot, and the foreign magician totally disappeared. *La Reginedda* quietly went back carrying the lighted candle. She climbed up into the bedroom and saw the sick young woman lying on the floor and revives her with perfumed water. Then for the next three days they drink the healthy broth and all the other good food that had been prepared for them. And they talk and they talk and the happy Princess looks out the window, where not one of the birds hopping, or flowers opening, or creatures and neighbors passing escaped her joyous eyes. In three days, the door is opened and the King sees his daughter restored. "Ah! My dear," he says to *La Reginedda*, "how many obligations I have to you! You must stay here with us so we can show our appreciation."

"Ah! but that is impossible. My father wanted to go to war to keep me from leaving. Now I'm sure he would do the same if I did not return." She stayed with them for fifteen days and then on leaving was given many riches and a great quantity of jewels. When she returned there was much rejoicing in the palace.

"They ended happy and content . . ." began Edmundo.

". . . and here we are looking for our true work," put in Agata, to conclude the tale with another story ending.

"What did you think of this story?" asked Edmundo.

"*Mamma Bedda, Mamma Bedda, stu cuntu . . . stu cuntu,*" sang out the parrot.

"Yes," said Costanza, offering Nello her arm, "I liked your story very much. You and Edmundo tell very fine stories."

"Treachery," sang out Nello.

Costanza laughed. "Treachery, Nello, is a strong word."

"*Traaaadiimentu,*" sang out the parrot nonetheless.

"Ha! Ha! Ha!" Everyone laughed at the bird, and Nello repeated, "*HaHaHa Traadimentu Ha Ha Ha Ha!*"

"Well," said Agata, "you tell a good story, my boy, but it's late and I have to start our meal. Will you eat in the study, Signura Costanza?"

"Oh! no, why don't we all eat here together." So during the preparations and until the last sip of coffee they talked of *La Reginedda* and magic. Agata and Costanza both told other stories that reminded them of Edmundo's story about magic and love.

"In my village," said Agata, "there was a married man who was given a love potion, a very strong one, and it caused a great deal of trouble for everyone. But the way people act nowadays, I think there isn't any work for these old magicians," she laughed.

"There is always work for good magicians," said Edmundo, smiling. And taking a coin from his pocket he did excellent sleight of hand to the delight of his audience.

"But there is magic and there is magic," said Agata.

"But you believe in miracles?"

"Don't confuse pretend magic with miracles. For one, you need a practiced hand, and if the audience doesn't know the trick you have deluded them; if they find out, they end up proper cynics. Most people are deluded sensualists, but don't ask me what they should be instead—I wouldn't know."

"But wait," said Costanza. "There is wonder when we watch Edmundo do his tricks. What if we knew the tricks and still believed in that wonder? Perhaps that is what a good magician shows: the possibility of magic while being deluded."

"That kind of magic," said Agata, "is how I feel when I am listening to the old stories. We could hear them all night and not bother ourselves about anything but listening."

"It's like holding magic apples in our hands."

"But they are also tricky," said Edmundo.

"Yes, tricky like our dreams," said Costanza as she accidentally shook the table sitting down.

At night

When the others went to sleep, Costanza went to her study to write her friend and colleague:

Dearest Friend,

How do your plans go for the magazine? L'Arethusa is a good name. I have not even thought about the article you wanted from me. Nothing comes. Right now you must not count on me for a contribution, although I must say that I am interested in looking into a story in Giuseppe Pitrè's folktale collection, I think it is in the first volume. If I remember correctly, it is the interior stories that are being told in this house. Yes, here. By whom? you ask. If you could see what I have unwittingly arranged, or I should say what has been arranged for me . . . A bit of both, perhaps.

A parrot, by chance, flew in through our one opened window (Yes, a parrot. Stop laughing!) and following it, its owner, or more properly its companion, a young sailor, Edmundo Patanè, from Sciacca. He came in through the door, not the window! He is a seaman on Captain Ruizi's Ulysses, a fine young fellow who has really helped us by putting our monumental provisions away and by keeping us good company, telling old tales.

Now we are all enclosed in this house together, living as a small family. Everybody here works and often together. I made a passable carciofi cu li piseddi yesterday. Our housekeeper and resident wise person Agata Milazzi from your coast, from Ninfa, is here keeping us well and well cared for, and loved. She has the rare talent of knowing how to present the right gift at the right time.

I am also doing passably with our agreed reading work, which is to say that I have been reading Basile and checking our notes for folk connections to the literary examples. But no critical writing yet. If the ashes are gently moved aside, who knows?

Please remember to write me about the Pitrè. "Lu Pappagaddu Chi Cunta Tri Cunti"? I can't quite remember the frame story of that one. Is it about a husband and wife? I know the motif of a parrot storyteller exists in Arabian, Spanish, even Asian versions. But I think the Sicilian one is not about marriage but about stories themselves. Please let me know, and if you can send a transcript I would be very tempted to compare it to this version.

Do you still hear the Sirens singing and the Cyclops roaring

on your coast? Memory's Daughters are shy and I ask them for
an indulgence. If only they would call. My ear is still attentive.

I am beginning to miss the coast and the sea there. The garden
here has glimpses of the harbor and the air is filled with the West.
The rain has been constant.

What is happening there? Have you heard any news from your
brother? I know you to be correct when you say he is a true cav-
alieri and you are a pugli, a madman. But then so am I a bit
mad, a bit pugli, a word from South India? I must stop using it
so casually, it's catching. I end as you began,

"You are well, I am well,"

Vales, valeo,

Costanza

Friday

In the garden of the Green Palace

In the garden the sparrows were noisy. It was the excitement of tag, catch, and voices. The cool air was shot through with sparrows. "Hot sparrows," said the Lady from the Sea, "come, swoop, and chatter." "*Chi, chi, chi,*" said life, "fly here, there, then turn in your place and fly in the opposite direction." "Oh! life! what true lessons," said the Lady of Beauty. "All mine know me by this living moment."

The garden was alive and going about its own business. The palm tree had breathed better; its old scaly skin and thick leaves were covered with dust, so much dust, so much extra human dust. It had lived a long time breathing the salt air which now filled the garden. This air came in waves like the sea itself; it came in undulating, unpredictable rhythms.

The actress tries again

The actress said a few encouraging words to the gentleman before hurrying away from the church steps. She was heartsick as she saw him stand so still and small beside the baroque figure of San Calogero.

Now late Friday morning she appeared at the door with another beautiful basket of out-of-season fruits in her arms. Today, she wore a simple China silk dress, a gray-tipped shawl, and a beautiful single strand of perfect pearls, something which gave her a bit more assurance than the ordinary kindly old woman. This was someone who might resemble Costanza's real aunt, she thought. But perhaps the pearls were a bit too much. And yet they had been the very thing on which she had built this genuine character. The instinct which she usually trusted now became her betrayer. There was something unsatisfactory about the pearls. What could it be? Oh! Yes. Wasn't there some strict custom about not wearing pearls before evening? Or was it permissible after five o'clock? Yes, that sounded right—five o'clock. It was not yet five o'clock, yet could that really be considered acceptable? Would Costanza note these now problematic pearls? (The streets were beginning to fill with people.)

All of a sudden her resolve fell, and she stood before the door with smarting eyes instead of the ease she knew she would need to carry the day. "That cursed parrot, I'd wring his neck if I could." It was amazing what this little anger did for her resolve. She banged the lion's head a bit too vigorously and heard it sound strangely hollow, as though it sounded in an empty house. She hit the knocker again. Her hand let go of the roaring lion on the now very dead doornail. She walked away. This is absurd, she thought as she turned back. And she was surprised to find Costanza smiling sweetly at her. She had been looking out of the convent window for a number of minutes.

"My daughter," said the actress. "I didn't sleep all night thinking of you." With these opening words she entered the large room, handed over another basket of extravagant out-of-season fruits and, warming to her performance, said, "I feel that you are the daughter I would have had had God graced me. Please do an old lady a favor. Protect your soul. You are surely in danger, my child. Come to church with me right now."

There was the faint smell of French lavender on frayed gloves as she took the basket, a scent which reminded Costanza of her old nurse. She could go out for an hour. What harm could come of it?

Again Costanza went to the old bureau, opened a heavy middle drawer, and took out a beautiful silk shawl.

The Gentleman waits
on the steps of San Calogero

Not more than three streets away on the steps of San Calogero, the gentleman waited. He waited with a full heart. Soon he would see her face again and hear the voice

that struck heavenly chords, although he had never heard
her speak a word other than *Ah*. His life would be changed
with her. Of course, he thought quickly, nothing might
come of it. In a few minutes, he would be speaking to her,
and then he would know if she too had noted him from
the window as he hoped. If nothing came of it, he had lost
little. Some joking from the lawyer, but he was sure his
friend had not spoken to the lady himself.

And then his heart sank. Again he felt himself slightly
unsatisfactory. Again he was about to withdraw. To whom
could he unburden his heart? His brother? His brother
always came to him with his problems. In his last letter he
had mentioned wanting some money for a Sicilian magazine he was publishing with friends. It was something his
mother would have approved, and yet it was quite a bit of
money. The thought of money reminded him of the substantial amount of the bet. Suddenly, he saw this bet in its
true light. It was not worthy of the lady, not worthy of his
own ethics. What was he doing? He would do better to go
to the *cappella* and pray for an answer in front of the beautiful mosaic of Christ, the *Pantocratore*.

He had created a trickery that was not for him. Not for
him. Not really right. No benefit from it. He sighed deeply
and walked up the church steps, feeling better than he had
in a long while. Perhaps tomorrow he would write his
brother about coming to visit him at the sea.

"*T*raitor! *Traitor!*" shouted the parrot, becoming wild,
pulling out his feathers, and lamenting in tongues.

Again he screamed, "Treachery, treachery. A story, a story, beautiful mother" (*Tradimentu, tradimentu. U cuntu, u cuntu, Mamma Bedda*). The frenzied bird pulled out feather after feather. They all went flying in a most disturbing way.

"I cannot come with you today, madame. I am sorry, but it's not possible. Thank you for your visit," said Costanza. And with these words Agata showed the woman out before another thing could be said.

"*U cuntu, u cuntu,*" shouted Nello.

"You noisy parrot," said the sailor, appearing in the doorway. "May I tell you another story?"

"Yes," they said together. ("Ah, I know this story, Edmundo," said Agata, "so if you need any help, you can count on me.")

"Agreed!" said Edmundo, putting on his jacket and sitting down at the table.

The Third Story

{ T e r z u   c u n t u   d i   l u   p a p p a g a d d u }

Now, once upon a time, there was a Queen and King who had an only child, a beautiful son who had no other enjoyment but to go hunting. Once he went hunting for a month to a far-away place. One late afternoon just before the sun set, he found himself walking in a woods. Now where do you think he happened to be hunting, and what do you suppose he found? In a small clearing in this wood, at the base of an old oak, lying amid the gnarled roots, he found a beautiful doll. As soon as he saw it he said, "I have finished my hunting! I'll turn back!" He picked the doll up gently and placed it in front of him in his saddle. Riding off at a trot, he said, "If this doll is so beautiful, imagine her owner." Along the way he said again and again, "This doll is beautiful! Imagine her owner!" And on the road he said, "*È bedda sta pupa! Cunsiddirati la patruna!*" He arrived at the palace and what did he do? He went to his bedroom, had a niche made in the wall with a glass fitted in front, placed the doll inside, and then looked at the doll twenty-four hours a day, saying always, "Beautiful doll; imagine her owner."

In no time at all this young man did not want to see or talk to anyone. He became so melancholy that his father brought together the best doctors in the realm. They came, they observed, they said: "Your Majesties, we don't know beans about this illness: it is neither in our books nor in our experiences, but you must look into his thinking about that doll." The King looked at his son; the son looked at his doll: "Ah! Beautiful doll; imagine her owner!" The doctors left the room compassionate failures, and the young man remained exactly the same, staring at his doll and yearning. Continuously he sucked the air and sighed, "This doll is so beautiful, imagine her owner." When the Queen saw that all her own wisdom was no good, she rang the Bell of Council. "Look at our son," she said. "Look at how reduced he has become. No fever plagues him, he has received no blow to the brow, but he is melting before our very eyes." And they lowered their tear-stained cheeks. "And our realm will be enjoyed by others," added the King with bitter irony. "Advise us!"

"Your Majesties, have you become confused? Don't you remember the young woman who saved the child of the King of Spain? And then against all odds saved another king's daughter? The King of Canicattì, we believe it was. Send for her. And if her people let her go willingly, fine; if not, we declare war and get her to come anyway!"

So a chain of ambassadors was sent, and while they were presenting their papers and telling their situation to the King, our Princess entered, and seeing the anger on her adopted father's face, she said, "Now tell me what is going on here? What is wrong, Your Majesty?"

"Oh, nothing, nothing, my daughter. It's just that yet another king is in trouble and wants you to save his son. I mean, this could be endless. He threatens war if you do not go. But I am willing to go to war," said the King, getting red immediately. ("You know the old saying, 'Better be red once than pale a hundred times silently,'" added Edmundo, shaking his head. "And both ways, red and white, could lead you to perdition quicker than the shake of a cock's comb," added Agata without missing a beat.

"Ah! Signura Agata, then you will like what the Princess said.") "Listen," she says, "don't make so much of this. I will go where I may help, see what can be done, and in a flash will return. No need for any more words."

"But now it's this king, then another queen, and I will no longer have any say over your coming and going."

"True," said our Princess, "I am now a woman and I don't need the protection I needed when I was a lost child. And, besides, Father, I have always had my own crown. Please, don't worry. I'll do what I can for these poor people, and I'll return in no time."

She embarked with her retinue and went for a long

voyage over the sea. After an uneventful trip of many days, they finally came to the palace of the dying Prince. Inside, in the great hall, all were lamenting and wailing, for the poor young man was near death. His soul was trembling on his lips. She entered his rooms and saw for herself that the Prince was eating himself up with every breath, lying on his bed saying in a whisper, over and over again, something she could not quite make out.

She drew the Queen and King aside, and while they walked back into the great hall, she told them, "You waited too long to call me! What were you thinking of? This is the very last moment. The very last moment! It is a grave situation. But let's do everything we can. Give me eight days. Make up a small bed for me in the ante-room. Prepare some good broth, some substantial food, and some salves that the doctors think appropriate. Then give me eight days. After this time, he will be well, or, I'm sorry to say, otherwise."

They gave her all the provisions; she entered the Prince's rooms, and closed the door behind her. She pulled a chair up to his bed and sat beside him. Next she put her ear down to his pillow to hear every word he was whispering.

"Ah! H . . . o . . . w . . . beau . . . ti . . . ful . . . is . . . the . . . d . . . o . . . ll. I . . . ma . . . g . . . ine her . . . own . . . er."

Finally, she understood his words and then followed his glance, now intermittent, for his soul was at his lips, and looking up, she saw, she saw *her doll, her very own doll!*

"*Mascalzuni* (rascal)! What are you trying to do here? Where did you find my doll?"

"Your d . . . o . . . ll? Is that tru . . . ly your doll?" he asked, coming back to life. And looking into her eyes, he said, "Ah! yes, that is your doll. I have finally found you."

At that moment she looked into his eyes as well. And so they had fallen in love.

Our Princess questioned him, watched him, listened to him, and sure enough she knew he was telling the truth. They were in love from that first sight. They sat and talked. At the end of the eight days he was well, and she was still in love with him. It was even better than finding lost companions, they said to each other over and over again. Look what I had to do to save you and to find my own Love, she said. She was an observant person, as we, by now, know.

When the Queen and King had the doors to the Prince's apartments opened, they found him alive and, more than that, in love. "Oh! I must give you my crown," said the Queen and the King together to the Princess. "Look at this! More crowns! We all can have crowns. Thank you, thank you, Your Majesties," she said, "but, believe me, I have my own crown and must in fact go back home to my own land."

So she went first to the family that had cared for and loved her all these years, and she told them that since she now understood how to get there, she must go home. And she took her leave with embraces and promises that they would all be together at the wedding. And as soon as they were able, the Prince Who Hunted Love and the Princess Who Helped Cure Impossible Cases married. And everyone was invited.

And they remained happy and content

And here we are looking for love.

After Edmundo said his ending, Agatuzza said, "My grand-mother used to remind us that 'They,' not we,' remained happy and content, forever and ever. The story doesn't promise us that *we* will live happily ever after. Our life changes moment to moment."

"That reminds me, *Signura*, you received a letter today."

"Where a . . . aa . . . aarrr . . . are you?" sang out Nello.

"They remained happy and content."

"And here we are without a cent," said the parrot, looking at them upside-down.

Later in the study Costanza read her letter:

> . . . *Costanza, get out of that decrepit house and join Felicia Coen and me. Felicia has been writing on the differences between the spoken and literary folktale in Sicily. We now have enough material to get out two issues, and my brother has finally agreed to back our journal. Everything is here: the food incredibly simple, and the house adequate. I think it's adequate. It seems we have only one sheet and no beds left, so the neighborhood is being searched for these provisions, "in order that your civilized guests can live in a little comfort" (but then my poor neighbor does not know the shocking fact that you have actually slept in the open air wrapped in your cloak). Felicia just reminded me to send you the tale you wanted. I am enclosing the very many pages of "Lu Pappagaddu Chi Cunta Tri Cunti" found in Pitrè (Biblioteca Siciliana IV). Are you going to write something on it? Of course, Friend, the sea is marvelous. Best of all, we have been hearing the Sirens lately. Yes, the Sirens have been singing again.*
>
> *Come soon, Costanza.*
>
> *Your amanuensis,*
>
> *Alfonso*

Midnight

Able to withstand the
Annunciation,
Angels come

The storm reached the harbor after midnight. In ten minutes the small fishing boats were whipped, and whoever had not taken precautions lost something to the sea. By one o'clock, in the garden the wind caught an old branch at the elbow, snapped and felled it, and the sound surprisingly reached the sleepers in the house. Edmundo had been dreaming all night of his old ship, but all the mates and seamen were strangers and he couldn't find Nello anywhere. Then he was standing at a closed door and he knew that there was a woman on board but he couldn't find her either. Agata awoke and took her rosary in hand and said the peaceful words of the Annunciation. Costanza was sailing on an ancient ship which cut the stormy sea like a knife, finally reaching a placid bottom, an absolutely "other world," and when someone called her name, she awoke. Nello dreamt something had moved beside him, and he awoke to the bright eye of a rat with a cuttlebone in its mouth staring at him.

Saturday

The Feast of Saint Rosalie, or the Ending

In all this rain, even the huge mountain which rose from the sea and hung above the city looked as though it were hunkering down. At first the garden in back of the Green Palace had rejoiced in the water, but when the rain had persisted for more than three days, small pools formed, the cactuses were surprised, and many of the figs of India fell from the laden cactus leaves. The small, unexpected movements of lizards stopped suddenly, leaving only the heavy and steady beat of the rain. Appropriate and uncomplaining as animals are, sparrows, along with the other birds and small creatures who lived there, found the best cover they could and waited and waited and waited. They waited. Even the stones lived within the watery life. How long would this rain last? The cats first crouched against the building, then sat inside the arcade of the cavaedium, then finally, soaked almost to the skin, moved on to an abandoned carriage shed. But their stomachs growled, and they were querulous with one another.

A large wet rat crossed the garden path nervously, turned its head as though it suspected someone's presence, then quickly disappeared down a small space between a broken hinge and a trapdoor frame, to run down a small flight of steps which led it to an ancient cave. The old cave had been incorporated into the palazzo's design, becoming a storage room for casks and demijohns of olive oil. Three months ago this family of rats, territorial and constant, after a few nights of noisy fights with strangers, had claimed their rights to the newly placed sacks of grains which had been hastily thrown into a garden outbuilding, and they had even licked a bit of olive oil seeping from the demijohn that had been put in the small underground room.

Like everyone else in the world, this family of rats had its own particular story. Their ancestors could be traced back to this very cave, where they had come after escaping from a sinking ship in Palermo's harbor. The rat crew made its way from the water to a rocky shore. From there they found a maze of tunnels and discovered the cave where their descendants lived for centuries up until the present moment. No one could dispute their supremacy. They were the current aristocrats of the old caves.

These tunnels and caves had served as a hiding place for prehistoric animals which no longer existed when Sicel families moved into them, and eventually they were replaced by Celtic tribes stopping on their migrations west, and then Phoenicians gave them up to Sicilians, who left them to Greek pirates, and they to Romans, and they to the Arabs, and they to the Normans, and so on to the Spaniards, and then to the French, and so on and so on, with numerous visitors and conquerors who passed by without entering them. At this moment, the rats and sundry other creatures were their sole inhabitants.

These rats had arrived in this particular place at a time when food was scarce, and many of them ended by dying from a terrible plague of fleas. This was 1625 in the human telling of the story, when the people of Palermo were consumed by the plague. Thousands upon thousands of people had already died, and there seemed no end to it—until Saint Rosalie paid an auspicious visit to a shoemaker.

Now, Santa Rosalia was a Norman Sicilian woman who left her aristocratic life to live as she desired—in the company of God. So she left the twelfth-century social life of Palermo to live her religious life alone in a hidden cave on Mount Pellegrino, high above the city. There, the legend is told, the holy woman lived as a hermit for forty years. But in all the years since then, no one had found her remains, until one night the shoemaker dreamt that Santa Rosalia had shown him where he could find her holy bones, and then and there she had promised him she would save the people from the plague. So he told the priest, who told the bishop, and they all found Saint Rosalie's holy bones in the place she had shown the shoemaker in the dream. Now, they went with the holy relics down to the church; and on the way the people hearing the news lined the streets to see or touch the reliquary.

It then happened that whoever touched or saw or was simply in the presence of the holy objects was cured. It was a miracle. It touched the old, it touched the young, it touched the rich, it touched the poor, it touched children and women and men. It touched foreigners and natives. All were cured. All believed the miracle after miracle after miracle. That is how the people of Palermo were saved and why Santa Rosalia became its patron saint and why there were three feasts celebrated in her honor. And since everyone looked forward to these great feasts, the people had been grumbling about the extraordinary rain—for tomorrow was the Feast of Saint Rosalie. In the Green Palace only Agata had seen the date and remembered. Imagine, she thought, to be in Palermo on the Festino di Santa Rosalia and not be able to go. But then you never really know what's going to happen.

This last month had been a difficult time for everyone: first the abnormal cold in a month known for its hot days, then the pouring rain with nights of high winds and sea storms, tempests for a full three days now, the ships in the harbor tossed, and the captains waited. It had been strange weather for the usual beautiful climate of the ancient city. The morning of the festino was overcast, but by midmorning a strong, hot wind from the South came in and with it a brilliant, clear sky. Suddenly, it was the kind of after-a-storm day that makes everyone glad to be alive. The sun was out and hot, animals and people began to move about, and activity down at the port was lively.

This was the day the sailor had to get back to his ship.

Edmundo finished putting his gear in order, swept his small alcove, put away the shining silver cage, picked up the green parrot's shells, and went out to the kitchen, found Agata, and told her he was leaving.

"We are also leaving. Where's Nello?"

"I brought him back to the ship late last night."

"Did the string hold?"

"It held. When is the *Signura* leaving?"

"She'll be following you out, by the looks of it. She's going to the port to book our tickets on the next ship to Catania. And so we go home, please God and the Blessed Mother."

When Edmundo found the lady's study, the door was already ajar, and Costanza was standing there with a portmanteau in one hand and a letter in the other.

"Signura Costanza, I have come to say good-bye. Agata tells me you are leaving too. So you are leaving right now, my lady?"

"Yes, Edmundo. We are leaving. I made up my mind last evening to take the next boat to Catania."

"May I accompany you to the port? I'm going to my ship."

"Fine, I would like your company, Edmundo. Where's Nello? Agata and I missed him this morning."

"I brought him back to the ship last night, with no difficulty at all. I'll get my belongings, and we're off."

For minutes, they did nothing but thank each other again and again for the work and for the good, loving company, two things not easy to come by in any age. With the courtesies over, Costanza moved to the huge front door and with some difficulty unbolted the old lock. Immediately, across the way, the lawyer called to one of his men, then put on his velvet vest and dark jacket, looked in the mirror to set the ends of his mustache. "Finally," he said, a smile beginning to spread on his wide mouth.

He saw her at the door, she was beautiful. Her black hair, violet eyes . . . he was just about to cross the street when the sailor appeared at the door, and just as Costanza was about to cross the threshold, the young man blocked her way with his body. What's he doing? What does he think he's doing? Ah! traitor! "Tino, come here. Where's your friend? We have more serious work to do than I had planned. And I need both of you to help me."

The great door was closed again and quickly bolted. Costanza was surprised at Edmundo's vehemence. "Edmundo, what are you doing?"

"Oh! Signura Costanza, I mean nothing but good by it. I found an incredible shortcut to the sea from right here at the house. We would go in the garden down some small steps that lead us to a dry tunnel that in no time will bring us to the port. The earth is solid and easy walking; I tried it out last evening with Nello."

"How exciting, Edmundo. The garden is full of surprises, like you." She laughed. "Good, let's go. I think I know where you mean," she said, going into the kitchen where Agata was sealing a package. "So the pirates are off, Agata. I will see you at the ship's office in the early afternoon. Since she sails this evening we must meet in time. Good morning, dear one!"

Just as the two were at the threshold to the garden, Edmundo turned to Agata and said, "Zi'Agata, will you bless me?" (*Zi'Agata, vosia mi benedica?*)

"A holy richness, full of virtue, son," she said, putting her arms around him (*Santu e Riccu, e chinu di virtu, figliu*). "May the Blessed Mother look over you and your ship and bring you safely to your home again, Edmundo."

Costanza, poised at the door, turned to Agata as well, "Will you bless me, Zi'Agata?"

"When you cross the threshold, *Signura mia*, you begin a new journey. So, my dear, I will tell you what my Grandmother Rosa used to say to me as I left her house: 'If any one tries to harm you, daughter:

May his eye turn to glass
and his hand to wax.' "
(*Occhiu di vitru; manu di cira*)

And then she added, "Bless you. A holy richness, full of virtue, daughter." Costanza embraced Agata and without a word quickly crossed the threshold. Edmundo, with his sack on his back and a lantern in his hand, moved ahead of her to the place in the garden which led to the tunnel. He lifted the trapdoor with its tangled mass of vegetation, recently wrenched aside, and they both slipped down into the dark cave. Here he lit the small lantern he had prepared, and to her surprise the tunnel stretched out before them. Some dark scurryings in the shadows. For differing reasons, neither mentioned them. It took no time for the two to reach a turn. All was going as he expected, but then there came a loud roar ahead and they stopped.

"What's that, Edmundo?"

"I don't know. I did not hear it last evening."

"Could it be the sea?"

"Hmm, no, the harbor should not be a roaring sea today. No, Costanza, it's something else."

"Let's go on."

He held his hand out to her.

"We're escaping!" they both said together.

"From some political intrigue," she added.

"Costanza, you could be escaping some political intrigue, something to do with fiery articles you wrote in a journal that is out of political favor."

"Are the articles any good?"

"I think they probably are."

"Oh! you're a critic as well as an escape artist?" she said, laughing. "Well then, what are *you* escaping, Edmundo?"

"What I have been escaping since I was born."

"What is that?" she asked him, standing still. His arm stiffened. She withdrew her hand. He turned to face her. The lantern between them cast thin, thin triangles on the wall.

"Listen, Costanza, I'm not a Patanè from your friend's family. I've never even spoken to her. My father is a fisherman who does the best he can. We are eight children, and my mother has been bedridden for years now. I am the oldest and do everything I can. I have been escaping poverty ever since I was born. The lady I mentioned is not in my family."

"Your name is Edmundo Patanè. I know your family."

"Yes, but between the noble name and our family's name there is a string of bread that crosses over to the Continent. I am sorry, *Signura,* but I knew no harm would come to you from me. I worried about someone else. Please believe me, I am honorable and would not betray you or myself for anything."

He looked at her clear eyes and felt he could see through them. She smiled and looked back at him. "Yes, but I knew who you were when I first opened that door. I have seen you with your family since you were a child. It wasn't because of the Patanè name and supposed connections that I opened that door, but because I already knew who you were. Come on, escape artist, let's find out what that sound is," she said, laughing, as she moved ahead of him into the last tunnel.

The noise was very loud now, a familiar rasping roar. "Those are human voices," they said at the same moment. They had reached the hidden entrance to the cave. She saw the light and was the first out through the small opening, and there—not ten yards away—was a great stream of humanity moving joyously and noisily before them. Once outside they were immediately pushed into the wave of people, laughing and shoving them on.

"What is going on?" they shouted to the people next to them.

"Are you joking?" shouted a man.

"Where have you been?" shouted a woman.

"It's the Festino di Santa Rosalia!" "Santa Rosalia!" "Santa Rosalia!" shouted two or three together.

"See, look! There! Right there!" They pointed.

Costanza and Edmundo were now a hundred feet from a slow-moving crowd following the palanquin bearing the beautiful statue and the huge reliquary displayed next to it. The jostling crowd with Costanza and Edmundo began to move faster and finally caught up to the palanquin.

"We are almost at the street, Costanza. We must turn here. Follow me," he said. Yet she disengaged her arm, threw back her head, and let herself be carried with the crowd toward the saint. He ran after her and caught up to her staring up at the statue of Santa Rosalia.

"Look, Edmundo, look at the beautiful expression on her face." Just as the crowd approached the crossroads, another wave of humans was joining the procession, and with it, in the forefront, were the lawyer and his henchman.

"There she is!" the lawyer shouted. "Tino, grab her, hold on to her. I'll lead her away." Tino moved forward, but just as he came within reach of her, an unexpected group of rowdy boys linked arms and barred his way. He lost her. But, by chance, Costanza was now within reach of the lawyer himself. He was excited. "Good! Good!" he said, taking off his gloves and pocketing them. They were almost at the street where he would carry her away. He pushed at the people in front of him with all his might. Just then Edmundo lost her, she slipped out of reach of his opened hand. The crowd separated them, and when he strained to catch sight of her, to tell her to turn left, he saw the lawyer. His heart became small.

"Costanza," he shouted. "Costanza!" He pushed against the great wave as hard as he could, but it was futile.

The people on his right pushed him back. "You poor, wretched thing, you lost your sweetheart." "*Mischinu*," one of them laughed. "I am not *mischinu*," he said under his breath, as a tremendous underwave caught him. "Costanza," he cried again as he lost his footing. "Costanza," he urged, but he could not get close enough to her and finally was inundated as wave after wave swept him away, even as he saw the lawyer moving closer and closer to her.

The lawyer was now only a few feet from her as he pushed the crowd with his shoulder. He was getting close. But as she came within his grasp, the palanquin, which had been turned so that the saint could face her old sanctuary on the mountain, now faced the bright sun and was flooded by its rays which at the same moment fell on both the statue and the head of the woman standing in awe. For a second Costanza was perfectly still and the lawyer confidently moved his hands out to grab her. At that very second the earth moved and the sun's bright rays now beamed from Saint Rosalie's amber eyes onto the lawyer's face, momentarily blinding him. Instinctively, he lunged for her all the same, but instead of her arm, his hands held a candle's burning flame and hot wax. Burned. His limp hands were burned. The thick candles that surrounded the Holy One continued to burn. He brought the waxed pain to his chest, shouting a terrible curse word which made the fellow on his left push him away. "You *maleducato*, uneducated lout!" he shouted back toward the lawyer as the crowd surged on. When the lawyer looked up from his burned hands, she was out of sight.

"Costanza," called Edmundo, reaching her while she stood leaning against a wall, down at the water. "How did you know to turn here?" he asked out of breath.

"I knew this was a way to the dock, and I knew if it wasn't the right street, at least I could find it from here. Besides, the crowd was turning away from the sea, and I did not want to get caught by them. Wasn't that lucky, to see Santa Rosalia like that?"

"Yes, lucky," he said.

In a few minutes, they were standing at the office of the sailing company, and Edmundo turned with a bow. "My lady, I have loved the time with you and Agata in the palazzo."

"I, too, Edmundo. Being with you and your quiet ways and your good stories has changed something for me. Your old story touched me, Edmundo. I shall not forget it or you."

They both stood silently for a moment. A catch of gulls flew up, tumbled and squawked and took their argument down the harbor.

"All I know, Signura Costanza, is that this time has been magic for me. I didn't know I could talk to anyone as I talk with you. I didn't know the heart and tongue could be in the same place."

". . . like a loved sister," she said.

"I don't know, perhaps," he said, dejectedly. "But I don't feel with you as I do with my sisters. But I have no right to talk to you like this."

"You and Nello and the stories gave me one last precious moment. I'm not sure what I will do, not exactly, but

I am going to see if I can help friends with some new work
that interests me. The work and I are just hatched. The
wings are still wet"—she laughed—"and besides, you and
I, Edmundo, just had an adventure at the Festino di Santa
Rosalia. Thank you, dear friend, for all your help. I have
been thinking how to help you and have prepared this letter for you to my brother. He is a ship's captain, and I
know he will be happy to meet you. I have already written
him about you. Please go see him whenever you want," she
said as she put out her hand to shake his. He took it and
kissed it. And they parted just as the door to the shipping
office opened and the ship's captain came out to greet her
warmly. Edmundo bowed and turned away, with tears in
his eyes, thinking of ports and parrots and a Bellini aria
and the fortunes of love for his young heart.

"Baronessa Patanè, how glad I am to see you. Where have
you been? Your friends say you have dropped off the face
of the earth."

"I've been in Palermo, Captain, but I'm going with you
to Catania."

"Wonderful! Wonderful! I have on my passenger list
the brother of a colleague of yours."

"Who's that, Captain?"

"Baron Vincenzo Lanza is going to Catania as well."

"My life lately is full of coincidences. I've just received a
letter from his brother, Alfonso Lanza. Lanza, Professor
Coen, Count Lizio-Bruno, and I are launching a Sicilian folk-
lore journal based on the work of Vico and Giuseppe Pitrè."

"Ah! the great Pitrè: *Fiabe, Novelle, e Racconti* (Folktales, Fictions, and Stories). Yes, how wonderful to see you again!"

In her cabin Constanza took off her gloves and sat down at the small table. That boy, that boy, she thought, agreeing to close himself in with us. No other way would have mattered. Even the stories said so. Tears fell on her hands.

It was, of course, the unseen world that interested her but only as it lived in the world's details, most especially when it revealed itself in visible words.

At   the   Green   Palace

"There, finally that little window is closed and I will be out of here," said Agata to herself as she climbed down from the table. But the table was so heavy that she did not even try to put it back. "Let the prince do that," she said, laughing. At the window she had seen a little, ragged boy waiting patiently for the lawyer across the way to open his door but everything looked closed and locked up there. Children and creatures can be so incredibly patient, she thought.

The luggage had been sent on a half an hour ago. She put out the lamp, placed it on the table, then reached for the open door. "Ah!" she said, crossing herself as she stepped out into the bright sun. "Let the others leave the house through windows or trapdoors or cellar stairs. As for me, I will go out the front door. It's by far the most direct way."

"My boy, please take these, a gift for your mother perhaps, will you?" she said as she reached the child, Tridicinu, standing at the lawyer's door, and he hurried forward to help her with the three unwieldy baskets of fruit that were, after all, out of season but still quite beautiful.

Months before, the rats, traditionalists at heart, had established within hours the best paths to their new provisions and had quickly included these paths in their nightly rounds. They knew to a grain how much they could carry and how long it would take to transfer the contents of the sacks to their own storehouses. Creatures of practice, they kept coming back every night at the same time to these underground paths, even after they discovered that the sacks were gone, suddenly gone, leaving only a mouthful of scattered wheat and the raw smell of their ghostly presence.

Rusina, Not Quite
in Love

The Rose

The man on horseback, sitting especially straight, did not look to the left or right of the highway, which after a while became narrower, eventually changing into a cart path, which in an hour gave way to a footpath, which all at once disappeared into a dark forest.

When he felt the reins slacken and then drop, the great bay went on for a few hundred feet, stopped before an enormous oak, and bending his neck began to graze. The man slid down, unbuckled the saddle, slipped off the bridle, found the horse's feed, and offered it. Then taking his own piece of bread he stepped inside the hollow of the tree to sit, eat, and close his eyes for a few minutes. The last thing he heard before falling into a deep sleep was the wind picking up. Within the hour it began to snow, and everywhere around him the silence of snow fell. He had been very tired: on waking hours later he remembered that he was lost, rubbed his arms and legs vigorously, stood up, and walked out from his fortunate shelter to find the late afternoon sun shining, the snow almost completely melted, and his horse standing a few feet from him. After whispering a few words to the horse, the man put on the bridle and saddle and mounted again and with a renewed feeling of hope found the road he could not find hours before. He was a rare person who accepted whatever place or condition he was in, whether from God, fate, or his own actions. This turning away from home to settle his accounts was simply the next step. He had gotten lost, had eaten a bit, slept, and was now ready to go. The cold hit him in the teeth and bones, and he quivered a bit, and for some unknown reason this quivering reminded him that he had not bought or gotten any of the gifts he had promised his daughters. A garnet grape necklace from India for the eldest and a blue silk shawl from France for the middle girl and what was it that the little one, Rosie, *La Bedda Rusidda*, had wanted? And with that question still bothering him, he arrived at his destination. The old villa, its name carved above the open gate, was exactly as the beautiful man had said. A sweet-smelling and peppery air enveloped him as he rode through and found himself in an unusual allée of rosebushes higher than his horse. Then he remembered, leaned over, and plucked the rose.

The Daughter and the Dawn

It was a black night, no moon or stars. Disturbing sleep, full of bits and pieces of dreams, dreams about houses, *houses she knew were hers but had strangely forgotten. In one dream she felt elated going through the old stone house, with its many rooms and surprising staircases; but then when she closed the front door behind her and had almost reached the bottom step, she had a presentiment that she would forget this house again. Next she was in a cart—the young sorrel standing completely still—a moonless night—impossible to drive on dark roads—but then she picked up the reins, and as the horse cantered through the marvelous dark, wherever the moon-shiny hooves touched the road became a wash of light.*

Before long they were in a village. At that moment, up ahead, she saw two men right in the middle of a crossroads, a bright lamp suspended from above lit them dramatically, like a scene in the theater, she thought. One man, with something white around his shoulders, was sitting in a chair, absolutely still, almost rigid, while the other man was standing behind him making small, mysterious gestures with his hands. When she got closer, she saw that the seated man was holding a large spoon over his left ear while the other was snipping and cutting his hair. She laughed out loud, but they did not hear or see her, and since she felt she was looking at something intimate, she turned the horse onto another road out of town.

Finally, she stopped; and when the eye of the brown-red mare, like a great sun turning, looked into her eyes, Rusina awoke and went to the window to see if it was yet dawn.

The night had been very still; then just before daybreak

a forceful wind swept the heavy clouds away, and out of the darkness a solid glow of red and purple light suddenly appeared in the sky, bringing across the infinite expanse giant lines of brilliant crimson mixed with thick strands of shimmering gold which stretched above and below the illuminated center. It was an amazing dawn, and all those in the neighborhood who were awake saw it and felt awe. A husband touched his wife's toes with *Come and look at this day!* In another house, a little child woke all her brothers and sisters with a fearful *Look! What does that mean? It's beautiful, that's all,* one of them laughed. A man whose wife had just died turned in their bed, awoke with a start, remembered for the hundredth time that she was gone, thought of his children, and with a heavy heart went to the window to open the shutters. The couple watched the brilliant show silently, then moved on to their chores and said no more about it. The children, pushing and shoving, fell into their beds again. The magic of this transformation gave the widower a moment of peace before he turned his back on it.

If they had all watched a little longer as the young woman leaning on the sill did, they would have seen the brilliant band suddenly diffuse and light clouds float above the pale remnant of what had been amazing only minutes before. These small and colorful clouds moved quickly above the horizon, going west, and then imperceptibly the dawn gave way to an ordinary morning of gray light with a hint of rain.

B e a u t y   A m o n g   t h e   S i s t e r s

The afternoon sun, almost out of the room's reach, played on the faces of three young women sitting in a small room. They were waiting for someone. Two were drinking coffee from delicate French cups on which an idyll of two shepherds was painted, while the third, exceptionally beautiful, sat fidgeting and occasionally whispering to herself, surely an unusual habit for a young woman almost eighteen. From time to time a large gray cat appeared at the doorway, looked in, then turned at the threshold to disappear down the dark hall. Rusina, the youngest sister—for the three were sisters, related by blood if not by sympathy—followed the cat's movements with interest. She almost rose from her chair, thought better of it, then sat down again but not before she inadvertently let out a kissing sound which meant "food." The cat turned in its tracks and ran toward her expectantly. Marta, the middle sister, was annoyed. "Go away! *Vatìni! Vatìni!*" she shouted, shooing the cat with her hand and upsetting a demitasse cup.

"Now look what you've done, you little bastard!" said Carmela, the oldest. "You do these things to spite us, just to spite us," she shouted, completely loosing control. "You are vulgar, *cafuna*, digging in filthy dirt. No respectable boy will ever want to marry you." But the youngest was used to this and sat with her lips pressed together and her thoughts wandering. "You're not even listening to me!" Carmela screamed.

"I hear you. I hear you. I'm not deaf, but you're going to make us deaf with your crazy shouting." Rusina shifted in her chair and faced the cat, who all the while, using her good cat judgment, had been heading for the food sound while ducking the waving hands around her. When the cat reached Rusina, the young woman got up, saying, "I'll let her out." Once on her feet, she felt nearly free and almost ran from the room.

"Wait a minute. I want to tell you something, little fool." Rusina stopped but did not turn around, looked down at the gray cat rubbing against her legs, and whispered, "You're a beautiful cat, Miciu, and I have something saved for you."

"Look at me! If Father does not come home with the money tonight, we will all be eating your cat's bread. You're spoiled and ungrateful. You're still a child, a little 'sweetheart' playing with life. You're not serious."

"Yes, I am. I'm very serious."

"Don't answer back!" shouted Marta. "And after you've taken that cat of yours out of here, come back to clean up the mess you've made. Now you see what you've caused? I won't be able to have that last sip." It was that last, delicious thick coffee and sugar left at the bottom of the cup which mattered so much to her. "The beautiful last sip," she crooned. "We two have sacrificed enough"—her voice picked up—"without you spoiling the little pleasures we have left."

This last was said with such conviction that it would have taken some minutes for a stranger sitting in the room to believe that she was now seeing the same sister scrape out the desired spoonful from the turned cup and hastily eat it before putting three new lumps of sugar into the cup and then refill it with steaming coffee from the silver pot which stood upon a little footed tray at her side.

Rusina left the room muttering to herself. As soon as she was in the kitchen, she took out a piece of chicken gizzard which she had hidden and held it out to Miciu, who took it delicately at the corner and dragged it away with a certain amount of cat urgency, purring loudly. The young woman looked to see if her father was coming, but nothing moved on the hot road. She sat down under her favorite tree, a wild fig with a gnarled trunk, and listened to her sisters preparing dinner. They laughed and talked the whole time, which sounded so normal, so ordinary and comforting from a distance—so human. It reminded her of the time, walking home at dusk from the village, when without meaning to she had stolen someone else's happiness. She happened to pass a house where a family was in the middle of a little celebration, probably someone's name day. And just as the grandmother came in with a plate piled high with fat pastries, the baby clapped its hands and squealed with pleasure, everyone turning to look, and the grandfather, who was holding the baby, kissed it and someone else clapped hands too, everyone encouraging this sweet explosion of joy. She could not help but stop for a second to look at them, and that's when it happened. In just a few seconds, her life had changed, and because of strangers she knew that this ordinary moment was possible. Now she thought, Look at that, you can't own anything; not even your own happiness belongs only to you. A thief could pass by in the night, steal it for herself, and you wouldn't even know that that pastry was gone! Just then she remembered the pastries were sfingi di San Giuseppe.

All of a sudden she felt cold and hungry, then looked up at the full moon shining in the cloudless sky one last time before she went to face her sisters. In the kitchen they were putting away the last of their meal and didn't look up as she walked in. She cut herself slices of bread and cheese and sat down at the table. "There's no sign of Papa." No one answered her. She finished her meal, washed her plate and cup, and was just about to go to her room when they heard the horse's hooves. Within seconds the front door opened, and an exceptionally handsome, well-dressed man came in to warm excitement and kisses.

The Father's Story

"**M**y daughters, these last two days I've been through purgatory. Purgatory! I have paid for many of my sins there. Please, dear ones, let us have something to drink," he said as he carried a rickety chair to the faded sofa, "and I'll tell you what happened since I left you." Rusina soon came in with the loaded tray.

"When I arrived at the port, there was a great confusion. A mob, unwieldy, yelling, pushing their way into the office. They were my creditors. Imagine the scene. They had heard, as we did, that my lost ship with its rich cargo had come into port. First, the captain and crew were paid, and then came the chaos. After only an hour, I saw that it was no use. Whatever I received went through my hands like water. I was Peter and they were Paul. All of it was lost. I cannot begin again as we hoped, my daughters.

"I was sitting alone at my desk when a man walked into the office. His face was so unusual that I became speechless. I must have stared rudely at him, but I could not help it—he was beautiful, truly beautiful. His eyes were the color of purple iris; he had shining black curly hair, no beard or mustache, and perfectly proportioned features. The most beautiful man I have ever seen. I didn't know a person could be as beautiful as that young man. A statue come to life. His manners were graceful, gentlemanly, slow. Seeing this perfection was so strong and otherworldly that my body quivered. I knew something I could not name had 'visited me.'

"'I am a messenger,' he told me in a beautiful voice, 'for the master of Selva Oscura. He would like you to go to the villa and make personal arrangements about the debt.' That sounded promising, so I agreed. It took me a day and a night to arrive at Selva Oscura. I was in front of an old villa covered with vines. I pushed open the ancient and heavy door and stood inside a narrow passageway. A panic came over me, but once I was out of this entry the feeling passed, and I was standing in a beautiful atrium with the calm sound of gently lapping water.

"After a very long time, an old gentleman came shuffling in and led me to a room where a bed was made up for me. 'Tomorrow the *padrone* will be here to speak to you,' he said. 'It's too late for you to travel. Perhaps it's best that you stay the night.' Just before saying good night, he lit a many-armed candelabra, and there before me was the most sumptuous table covered with many fine dishes. And then I realized that in this simple room everything was luxurious. The carvings on the chair were of the most amazing craftsmanship, and there were tapestries covering two walls, scenes where only women were the hunters and both men and women tended the land, and the land was like the old days, filled with tremendous variety of plants and trees. In the middle of a dense wood was the stag in his element. There was no scene of dogs or capture, but in the last panel was our Blessed Mother holding one hand to her heart and with the other offering us a golden thread. It was something to see, and afterward I slept and dreamt a beautiful dream, which I cannot remember.

"In the morning the old gentleman came in bringing me some breakfast. He opened the shutters and the room was flooded with beautiful sunlight. I felt more optimistic. From the window I saw a lovely garden and beyond that a wood as far as I could see. When I turned from the window to ask the old one when could I speak to the *padrone* of this marvelous place, he was gone and again I had no answers. Making the best of a glorious day, I went in search of the door that would bring me outside into that garden. The place was a labyrinth and no amount of guessing helped me out of it. Finally, I stopped, closed my eyes, and when I opened them, by luck found a door that led me outside. What had seemed a small garden from my window now stretched out before me for hectares and hectares, an exquisitely planned area with huge cypresses and water coursing down the sides, continuously flowing. A bounty I could not have imagined in those barren, rugged mountains. I kept walking in this paradise until I came to a large greenhouse. You know how surprising the temperature always is in those places. There were rows of plants growing in orderly disorder like no greenhouse I had ever been in before. In the last aisle, amid a row of deep yellow roses, I saw a gardener kneeling at the foot of a fragrant plant. He was dressed in suede of soft brown and green, but he wore no shoes, neither sandals nor slippers. He blended in with his earth surroundings so completely that I did not see him until I was almost upon him. It went through my mind as I walked up to him that I might get some useful information from him about the road to the city, when unexpectedly from where he knelt he said, 'Right from the gate, then right again at the crossroads, and you are on the road to the sea.' I had not yet spoken to him. How had he known my question? His speech was odd. I felt he might not be ordinary.

"At this point he stood up and I was startled. He was a mountain of a man, Mongibello itself, and when he turned his face toward me I shuddered, for he was so ugly I could not look at him directly. Daughters, this is discourteous and I know it, but I could not help averting my glance. As I said, he was beastly, with small unblinking eyes that mercifully never looked at me. He had a full beard and hair over his brow, and although he stood facing me, his gaze always looked slightly away from my own. His grizzly red-brown hair was unkempt; his chest was huge but his shoulders small and narrow. His gardener's hands hung down like a great beast's paws. He looked powerful, sorrowful, and even angry. His emotions were unmistakable, and I felt them immediately. We stood like this awkwardly for a minute or two until he spoke.

"'You people owe me a great deal and you never pay,' he said in a low and agitated voice, 'and I'm tired of waiting. Pay me now. You are all ungrateful.' He had the most horrific *rrrr*s in his speech. At first I didn't know if he was growling or a native of the Continent. I answered him politely, and finally he turned, looked away, and in a quiet voice invited me to luncheon with him. He spoke in our tongue so beautifully that then I knew for certain that he was from the Island, from these very mountains of the interior, from the *umbilicus*, as your grandfather would say. What could I say but yes? You can imagine my surprise when I understood that this gardener was my creditor and the *padrone* of this unusual place.

"He lead me back to the house by a different way, and I was astonished when we entered yet another hothouse filled, he told me, with a variety of bulbs from our Island that I had not seen since I was a boy, certain hyacinths and crocuses and all kinds of colorful lilies, their fragrances so powerful that I was overwhelmed with the sweetness. Cyclamen, wild and cultivated, were there, and he also showed me a small patch of orchids. 'Hidden, always hidden places where wild orchids grow,' he said in a whisper. There was even an entire room given over to wild rosebushes, which even I know are unpredictable. These he passed slowly, turning now and again to look intently at something which I could not see, being neither a gardener nor a woodsman. He called these flowers and plants by names I did not know, perhaps personal names or even very old names no longer used or heard. Once he stopped to touch a thick rose branch so delicately that I marveled at his ability, considering his huge hands and the proliferation of thorns. Sometimes he stopped and so I stopped a little way behind him to watch as he would bend down to fix this flower, that stem. He never pulled or cut anything as I have seen gardeners do. He stooped as he walked as though his delicate legs were a nuisance to him. Yes, as though his legs were a nuisance to him. He dressed in breeches, as I told you, and at the door he slipped on a pair of boots with no bending or difficulty and lifted his green hunting jacket off a hook and put it on before entering the house. I caught a smell like mud and old leaves that comes before the orange trees bloom in early spring and the earth is still winter wet and smells everywhere like this—not altogether unpleasant, the word *dank* comes to mind, but on reflection I would rather say *moist*, like the earth around a woodland spring where earth and water are so intermingled it is hard to know where one begins and the other ends.

"He led me to a stately chamber and asked me to sit next to him at a massive table, set with a fine cloth, and as soon as we sat down my old friend came in, all smiles, carrying a tray of finely sliced bread with *companaggiu*, sliced cheeses and salami and plates of green olives and small black ones that were very tasty, and there also was a large plate of caper blossoms on their stems. They were excep-

tional, thin delicious flowers that had been prepared in a
light vinegary bath. I was served plate after plate of the fine
meats and vegetables but Signore B. took only a large por-
tion of the capers, slowly eating each flower off its stem,
one at a time, working down the row intently but gently,
until he had eaten every one. And when he had finished
them, he wiped his lips and drank a sip of the superb wine,
then put down his spotless glass, picked up another stem,
and started snipping off flower buds from the top and
worked his way down the stem again intently but delicately, until he had finished that one as well. I, too, enjoyed the
capers, following him as well as I could. Another pitcher of
his excellent wine came, and I was beginning to feel light-
hearted. We ate without making conversation, and afterward he looked up and said rather unexpectedly, 'When are
you planning to pay me? You owe me a good sum of gold.'
There beside my plate was a paper I had not seen before,
with my name and a sum. My daughters, the sum was huge.
'Sir,' I said, 'my daughters and I are reduced to a small rent-
ed farmer's house in the country, where rocks are more
plentiful than bread. And if it weren't for my youngest
daughter we would be living in the poorest way.' 'How's
that?' he asked me. And I explained how we left the city in
a poor and dejected state, and then, I don't know why, I
started to tell this stranger about *Rusidda mia*, who was the
only one of us cheerful about starting a new life. I said,
'Rusina is like her mother, God rest her soul, who had a
gift for making things out of nothing, out of what others
cannot see or imagine.' 'What kind of things does she
make?' And with that I told him story after story about

you, child, and I could have gone on for hours, but then I saw him smile a sly smile and I stopped, realizing I had already said too much. 'I have a solution for you and your family,' he said. 'If Signurina Rusina is willing to come to the villa as companion to my old aunt and uncle, then your debt will be canceled. Here in this place we would welcome your daughter.' But, *Bedda,* I said I would not send you, and he got me to promise that I would at least ask you. So you must think carefully if you want to go to work as a companion to these old people. I told him clearly that I did not want you to leave our house.

"He said to me, 'I assure you here she will be safe with us. We are a respected family in our district. Ask and you will find this out. But I know that Signurina Rusina is what our dreary household needs. Give her the choice and I believe she will come.'

"He left me with those words. And now I have told you more or less everything that happened."

"Just for now, Papa, it is all that has happened just for now," Rusidda said. "And since you said it was purgatory, then heaven is in reach."

"Or hell?" piped up Carmela. "Hell is another possibility," she said as she folded her napkin carefully and placed it beside her plate.

Rusina's Story

That is where my father's story ends and where mine begins, well, of course, not quite. Because it seemed that I was paying my father's debt, the moralists will say, "This is not right, not right at all," but I ask you not to judge my father too quickly. My great-grandmother and grandfather inherited debt as did my mother and father and on and on, for what child does not inherit parents' debts? Debts from character and disposition. Debts from unlived life, sickness, unremembered dreams, poor work, hungry stomachs, stingy imagination, or little love. It is a rare and blessed child who comes into this world without debt. Besides, when duty and love are two sides of the same coin, then payment is not a burden. All this aside, I knew that I was in this situation not only because of some personal or cosmic plan of debt and payment but also simply because of my father's tongue. He was a hopelessly convincing story-teller, so when he told the Master Gardener about me I might as well have been packing my things.

The day before I was to go I opened a large empty trunk and began filling it with my assorted clothes and keepsakes, throwing them in with abandon. My sisters, having the exquisite ears of dogs, heard the trunk move and came running in. "So you think these are yours, you stable shit. These things were all ours before you got hold of them." What a joke that was. The miserable rags would-n't even fit them anymore. "Truly, truly, elegant manners," I mumbled. They came back with "*Stronzaccia*, big shit," and I with, "You both should know! Your mouths are the biggest pieces I've ever seen." With that they both opened their hands toward me and two tiny china teacups fell, shattering at my feet. I smiled and turned away. In those days I was a case of good-bad, bite the air and run away. Yet no words I ever muttered or actions I ever took stopped them. They continued to argue over every scrap, assuring me again and again that nothing I was taking was mine. They were righteous one minute, then argumentative the next, telling me I was a "lazy sinner, a powerful cynic, an ungrateful sister." Although it wasn't true, I rather liked "powerful cynic"; I don't know if it was the "powerful" or the "cynic" that pleased me. I saw them as stupid and vain and altogether uninteresting. But still they were my sisters; and before this chance to leave home I had accepted my misery, as every child does, exactly as it was. I always imag-ined a way out but nothing you would call probable. By midmorning they had dragged the trunk away empty. So when my father came home I was standing there with bare hands, taking only the clothes on my back and my mother's frayed traveling case. This old portmanteau was made of beautiful pale tapestry, tattered and bound by strong cord, and since I had lost every rag and broken cup, it carried all that I really needed. Besides, I am a coward in small things so I never fight over them. To be fair to my sisters I'm sure that I annoyed them by everything I did and said, by my very existence. But I must say it here: this need to be fair even to my enemies is a serious character flaw in me, which has always gotten me into the worst trouble. "Good-bye, sisters," I sang under my breath. My father was another matter.

Ever since I can remember, my father has called me "Beauty." To call someone "Beauty" may sound unusual, especially if they are not terrifically beautiful, which few people are, but Sicilians often call people they love *"Bedda"* or *"Beddu."* We call the Blessed Mother *La Bedda Matri*, the Beautiful Mother. Beauty and love are always on our lips. "When we say '*Bedda*' or '*Beddu*,' we are saying something very old," my grandmother used to say. "All gifts come from a place we do not will. Beauty and love come from this place." From the beginning, my father and I knew each other without explanations. When I was little my mother often said laughingly, "You two are a pair of aces back to back and from the same deck." This does not mean we were exactly alike. We were not. I did not tell my life as a story as my father did. He told stories about everything and I loved listening to them. We both loved reciting poetry.

He was extremely brave, saving strangers, animals, and family in the order they came across his path. He was a creative mixture of innocence and wisdom, delighting especially in old ways and proverbs. He was always full of hope, saying "God closes one door and opens another" when my sisters carped about their dresses or lack of social position. With him I felt happy, safe, joyous, but when he wasn't home I found peace by escaping to the garden. His imagination was romantic and social, he was a man's man and a woman's man, both old and young loved him. I am not exaggerating, I never do. He sang songs well and easily, played cards, loved nature and animals fiercely. My imagination was more private and solitary, more darkly cloudy. "Don't pay attention to your sisters, they don't know what they're saying," he'd encourage innocently. He never saw my misery as different from his, which he could abide as long as we were together. My father was not perfect and I never imagined he was, but then neither am I. When he called me *Bedda* he was saying I was beautiful to him.

Finally the time came to leave. My father met me at the door, picked up my case, and carrying it out told me that he had made further inquiries about the Master Gardener. Among ourselves we consider secrets unhealthy, and I knew that my father, asking casual questions, would get back serious answers. Within the day the word came back: the inhabitants of the villa—an old man and woman and the Master Gardener—were well known in the district as honest, decent, and harmlessly eccentric. Since we are an island of eccentrics, no one pays serious attention to the term. The Master Gardener was called a wild card from some medieval deck. He knew wildflowers from the center of the island so well that he even knew their genealogy. He had saved two kinds of wild grasses from extinction. "He loves plants better than people," more than one person reported. The village children were already making stories about the place, and the old wags were shaking their heads. They always added that he was generous with his food and money, "*È generusu, assai generusu.*" The very worst thing they said about him was that he was ugly, truly ugly. They called him *Il Laidu* or *Il Bruttu.* "He's so ugly that you can't even describe him. He's so ugly that he never leaves the villa. He's so ugly the sun hides when he comes out." I found all of this interesting but I hoped not too interesting, for although I never said a word to my father or sisters, my heart had a little *tremolo* when I thought that I would soon be living among strangers.

"Go!" my sisters said. "Go and good riddance! We won't have to see your face, you dry-hearted ingrate. Go!" There was no doubt that I would go. I could taste my life away from them.

The road to the villa was long and difficult. My father and I arrived at dusk. Even in the fading light the villa was imposing, a huge building of a very old style that I had seen in ancient history books. "Ah! Look, *Bedda*, the door is ajar again," my father said, pointing out details that verified his story. He knocked politely ("as if one could ever really knock politely on a closed door," my father said, turning to me). The huge carved door slowly opened, and before us was a man who had the most inquisitive eyes. He was all smiles and for a welcome he said, "Ah! So you've both come. How delightful!" And then addressing me he asked, "What is good for the nose but bad for the fingers?" He didn't expect an answer to his riddle, which I, of course, had guessed to be "rose," and when he gestured for us to follow we all three went single file through a narrow passageway which led into an open courtyard in the center of which was a pool filled to the top. There were rooms around this pool. He showed me mine and then went off with my father. I was left with my mouth opened. My room had a sparse rich simplicity I had never seen before. I was struck with the beauty and usefulness of the few objects that were in the room. At my bedside there was a remarkably decorated water goblet with scenes from the flight of Arethusa painted vividly around it. The first scene was of Arethusa fleeing from the river god Alpheus, he pursuing her so closely that any minute he might touch her neck; then of the wood goddess, in answer to Arethusa's plea, creating a cloud to envelop the nymph and hide her from Alpheus; then of Arethusa inside the cloud, and at her feet, the flowing stream she herself is becoming running off; next of the ground cleaving and of her plunging down into the earth; and the last of Arethusa in the form of a nymph emerging from her deep fountain at the edge of the sea, offering water. An upside-down cup fitted over the narrow-mouthed opening, so that when I removed it and the pretty cup was sitting neatly in my hand I saw painted at the bottom a flowing spring at the edge of a marshy inlet. When I poured the water from the tumbler into the cup, it filled the spring—and I was drinking from the sacred fountain of Arethusa itself. This bold crossing from the imagined to the real moved me to quiet tears.

Soon the old gentleman came to show me to a large dining room where my father was waiting for me. We ate alone and in spurts of cheerfulness and gloom. "Let's go home. Come on, *Bedda*, let's go."

And each time I would say, "No, I want to stay." I had never seen any human place so luxurious and abundant.

"Do you like this food, *Bedda*?"

"Yes, but if I get tired of it, I can show them how to make my bitter chicory soup or, for a treat, my Sunday sauce of fried chicken hearts and tough gizzards over my badly made pasta."

"Don't say that. It was a fine simple dish." Irony was not my father's suit. After this feast we played cards until a number of clocks began chiming, and at midnight we left each other in a passable mood. After saying my prayers, I fell into a troubled sleep under that beautiful *cuttunina.*

The next morning while at breakfast the old aunt and the humorous man who had welcomed us came to introduce themselves as if we were at the most normal of villas. As is our custom, I called them Aunt and Uncle, which pleased them. Her name was La Zia Graziella and his Lu Ziu Luiginu. She chatted with my father, saying she was so glad to see a young woman in the place. "My dear sir, old age is a carcass," she said. (*La vecchiaia è 'na carogna.*)

"Only for those who live that long," the old man added slyly. (*A cu ci arriva, a cu ci arriva.*)

"Youth and beauty are great treasures," she added, smiling toward me. By ten o'clock my father's carriage was ready. We walked arm in arm to the gate, where after a great embrace and many loving words my father left, tears in his eyes. I stood stunned like a lost or abandoned child. And for the first time that I could remember my heart broke. Until that moment I had trusted parental love completely as I had trusted nothing else, not food or clothes or shelter, for I had known deprivation and vicissitudes in these but never in love.

My father's last words to me at our parting were meant for reassurance but gave me none. "If you want to come home get word to Pino. You remember where he is working?" Yes, I nodded, but I knew I would not call Pino, an old neighbor of ours who had come to work near the villa. In the night I had understood that this leaving was a kind of death, and suffering it I was already beginning to feel resigned to it. This resignation was not a mask; it was the blessed bread which nourishes courage.

I have never clearly understood why or how things change, whether by great leaps or by quiet standing still. When things change, the small part of me is always surprised while the larger part of me is not. The everyday part of me expects things to go on as they did the day before, no clothes of my own, hand-me-down rags, my sisters complaining and nagging me to death—who cared? What did it matter? Nasty words, what did they matter? When our father was away, I felt blissfully happy outdoors, where my sisters never followed me. Their words *cafuna, mascalzu-na, brutta, sciocca, bastarda* did not bother me since the description was so false I always felt they were talking about someone I did not know. But there was one word, *vagabonda*, in which I reveled. I knew from an early age that my path would not be fixed, and on my walks I called myself *vagabonda*.

It was the world of dresses and cups and food and angry outbursts that I did not trust. Unlike my sisters, I never worried whether the dress tore or the cup broke, although I felt truly sorry for things, as though in loving them even a little I could see that they also had a life, even the strangest of objects. I learned about this before I knew the smallest separation between other things and myself. Once when I was very, very small, I had fallen on a stone path and a harmless crusted knee resulted. I had cried because I was sure that my mother was going to scold me for being a tomboy and having run and fallen and gotten my dress dirty. Instead she had not said much about either the torn dress or the knee. The resultant sore that covered the wound was almost as big as half my knee, and I got so used to it I thought it was to be part of me forever. So when one day I saw this scabby old friend fall off, I picked it up, crying, and with deep sobs I went to the dining room, where my grandmother and grandfather and mother and father were all sitting together. "Put it back!" I cried. "Put it back!" They first tried to reason with me, then to console me, but I cried and cried, something I never did even as a child. I don't remember who came up with the solution, maybe my father or grandmother. "Here, let's save it on top of this cabinet where it will be safe and you will know where it is." At that moment I felt glad and calmed and stopped crying, but I knew, absolutely knew, that my old friend was not going to be there forever, and I had learned something of value which all the adults in the room already knew.

There was something else I experienced in that room, a feeling that had changed things, a benevolent spirit that existed among them. Yes, I knew that the adults could solve things, that they knew about the world, but I also knew that I was safe among them and that they would teach me how to live properly among things. Perhaps it was because I was so small and still felt the world so completely that I could recognize this spirit in the adults; it was delicate and serious and it had made all these smiling elders happy that I stood among them no longer weeping. It was this spirit I often noted later that helped me to jump, leap, move—and it had now carried me away from home.

The Villa and Its
Inhabitants

In the cold night
Way, way up
Almost out of sight
The small stars hissed

The windows and doors not locked or shuttered were open to the night,
as though nothing needed to be closed here. There was no danger, it said,
not here, not there, or anywhere near. The old house was so simple, a
series of squares and rectangles leading one into another easily and in
the center an open court, the roof opened to the sky, its sloping sides
spilling rainwater into an impluvium, which in turn filled the house
reservoir. In a week of autumn rain the pool was sparkling, the top lay-
ers moving now with the slight wind.

I lived my first days at the villa in a kind of dream, partly because I was on my own in a beautiful magical place where every necessity had been thought of and partly because I saw no one, neither the old man nor the old woman, and I could dream and explore to my heart's desire. For the first time in my life, I was not constantly scolded so I felt a sudden elation that had no time or geographical limits. Each morning there was some small thing left for breakfast in the kitchen, and in the afternoon and evenings when I went into the dining room everything was prepared and left for me in sumptuous plates and steaming trays. At night in my room I found a plate of fruit and biscuits and my Arethusa fountain always filled with fresh water. On the third day I discovered a little note in a scribbled hand hidden under the very full biscuit tin: *The time to take cakes is when cakes are passing.*

I loved my room for its sparse beauty and, child that I was, because I found everything I needed for my comfort there. I mean for me especially. I'll give you an example: there was a small case and in it there was an old and beautifully made book of L'Abbate Meli's *Fables*. To these I added a well-used dictionary common in my grandfather's day (*Il Nuovissimo Melzi* had actually been his) and a book of poetry by my uncle Vincenzo Guarnaccia. That night I saw that three books of medieval Sicilian poetry had been added, next to which I placed my four empty notebooks and a porcelain figure which had been my mother's of a woman seated in a Roman chair reading a book, an object of sentimental value my sisters believed broken. When I returned to my room, there were eight more books on the chest, including a beautiful set of encyclopedias with hand-colored illustrations, Ovid's *Metamorphoses*, and an old edition of Christine de Pizan's *The City of Ladies*. If this Fibonacci series (every number is the sum of the two previous ones: 1, 2, 3, 5, 8, 13, 21, 34 . . .) was to continue, it would have to be one-sided since I did not have the thirteen books needed to continue the game.

There was wonderful play with my clothes as well. I had worn my one dress, having done the best I could with it, taking off the collar and cuffs on the second night, and when I awoke they had been washed and ironed and already sewn back on. In the evening of the third day, I found in the armoire two skirts and three shirtwaists in lovely grays and tiny Swiss dots which I would have chosen myself if asked, and they all had my name embroidered on the inside, *Rusina*, in red embroidery silk. Even my silent wishes were noticed. Coming home one afternoon from a long climb, I spied a pair of trousers drying over a laurel bush and thought how useful they'd be. The next morning hanging in the armoire were two pairs of pants, two shirts, and a green jacket. Forgive these foolish details, but who among you, male or female, has not wished that you could open a drawer or armoire and find exactly what you needed, no, would have chosen if you had had the chance or sense. Well, anyway, there it was and each day I would discover some other place in the villa or the surroundings that was more beautiful than what I had found the day before.

The plan of the house was an old and simple one. The entrance, a kind of short tunnel, led you to an open courtyard and my room was off this. It was a simple geometric plan of rectangles, the empty spaces all flowing into rounds of new rooms so that all the public spaces were connected. Straight back off a colonnaded garden were the private quarters, and at the end of them was a room which had a great oven with a small couch on one end and a big cooking stove with three places for pans on the other and then in the center a rather old-fashioned table and chairs.

It was very kind of them to give me these days free to explore; it was my first time completely alone in the world, and while at times I looked about cautiously, this sense of sublime care and peace while being absolutely alone was new to me. My own habits, either from character or from situation, suited this time, and I wondered if it was their plan or happenstance. Finally I began to miss the Aunt and Uncle's company and felt eager to begin working as their companion, although when I had asked if they would like me to read to them or help them, they giggled and shook their heads no.

On the fifth day after breakfast I went to the kitchen determined to find them. Where were they? Someone had been preparing all my food. If they were anywhere, they would be in the kitchen. The room was completely still and empty. In the corner next to the oven was a huge heap of black rags covering the couch. Among the patchery was a large piece of tapestry which so caught my eye that I was trying gently to lift it out from under the weight of its con- freres when I was startled by a pair of blinking eyes look- ing at me.

"Do you want something?" asked a familiar voice.

"No, not particularly," I answered, letting go of some part of human anatomy covered by the piece of tapestry. I think it was a hand.

"Good! I thought perhaps you had come to ask me to dance, taking my phalanges (my fingers, dear) like that, but I think it is much too cold to move from here, let alone dance," she said, sitting up. And I saw that it was Zia Graziella covered in what seemed like everything she owned. "On days like this I sit near the oven and prefer to do nothing but think." Now I saw two ragbags move, becoming a pair of fur slippers, which after much shuffling rested on the marble floor. "Autumn begins the time for longer thoughts, which gets you ready for winter, which has the longest thoughts of all."

"I'm sorry to have disturbed you, Aunt."

"I should hope so. At my age disturbance is either cat- astrophe or great pleasure, and I suspect this is neither. However, now that I am disturbed from my long thoughts"—but I never heard what the consequences would be since the old man came in, saying, "Long thoughts, long thoughts, my foot. A short thought in a long winter is enough for anyone—especially for you, Sister."

"So you would have them think, but then *you*, Brother, have no diploma as I do. Two you know, I've got two, which certainly gives me the impression that I could sustain one. Since two of course is the greater number."

"And what of it? And what of it? I suppose next you'll be telling me it's the right time to fetch water and start sup- per when it's the *wrong* month as usual and that last fool of a crested woodpecker is still out in the orchard calling for his lady love. Time is gone and even the numbers have had salt thrown on them. They can't grow, you know," he said turning to me, "not with all that salt thrown on them."

"Poor things, poor things, it's sad about the numbers, but they never could take care of themselves. Of course if they keep acting irrationally then people will throw salt on their tails! But then it is hard to turn from your own nature no matter what people say or do. Certainly I wouldn't."

"Let the numbers defend themselves!" said the Uncle in a declamatory manner.

"Oh! What an idea, Brother! You put me in mind of Emperor Honorius' message to the Western Cantons when you speak like that. 'Let the cantons defend themselves.' Sad affair, sad affair. All those poor women burying their silver spoons hoping to return to their homes some day. They never did, never did. The cantons could not defend themselves, Rusina. I hope the numbers will do better. But we still have your problem, Brother, with the woodpeckers singing out of turn. Ah, but woodpeckers! Why are they playing their timpani? It can't be, dear Brother, for it is almost winter."

"I think, Sister, they are looking for a little *appoggiatura* to lean on, so to speak."

"I doubt we can help them with their musical compositions, graceful as they are. No, we have other work to do now that we have a *young lady* in our home. Now that this child has come, what are we to sing to her, I ask you?"

"True, Sister, what are we to do? She has hardly a wooden spoon or a book to her name and surely she can't stuff artichokes correctly or bake little cakes like Bishop's Buttocks, Little Hats, or things like that. True? True?" the Uncle said, becoming excited with anticipation.

"I believe you mean Chancellor's Buttocks, Brother."

"Bishop's, Chancellor's, what does it matter? The shape is the same, so there!"

"That's exactly where you are wrong. It matters to everyone eventually. It matters. Bishops and chancellors are *not* the same thing. But let us not debate the case anymore before that awful selfish ad hominem comes to the kitchen and it is too cold to keep that door open! It's cold enough as it is." Then turning once more to me she said, "Tell us, Child, why are you here? And what can we do to make you happy? And even more important would you tell us *what it is you do anyway?*"

"I'm here to keep you company, I believe."

"Keep us company?" they both said together.

"How strange. No one has ever done that before," he said. "It will be a novelty."

"Or a catastrophe," she added smiling.

You can't say that I wasn't warned, but you see they were not so much mad as daft or cranky. Eccentric, as people had told us. Zia Graziella and Ziu Luiginu, as I now called them, were a wonderful family for me, but as for my keeping them company, I can't say that I did much. I got accustomed to jotting down their conversations afterward, and soon I could remember them whole as you can remember new and exciting things. These little writing books were also useful for drawing objects that I couldn't describe. Each day we ate our midday meal together; then in the evening I ate a light supper alone in the dining room, afterward playing the spinet that appeared in the corner one day with *Rusina* painted on it. And so for the entire first month I lived a happy idyllic life. I never saw the Master Gardener, though, and I was very curious. He was nowhere to be seen inside the house—although one afternoon I did see an enormous shape like a bear carefully study its way through a field, turning stones. I knew at once it was the master of the place. Its power and purpose inspired awe, for it could do what it wanted. I watched it for a long while until it disappeared out of my sight.

A few weeks later, after much of the harvest was already in, the old Uncle and some neighbors picked the grapes from the small vineyard. He waited until the last possible minute for they needed a little rain he said, just a little. I too had helped, for the work needs many hands and I learned to be good with the cutting knife. The immense grapes were bursting with sweetness, and the small birds got drunk with them. Everybody said the Uncle was wrong to have waited so long. We were all frantic to get the grapes picked and in, for by the end of the week it had begun to rain in earnest.

One night while I was listening to the rain fall outside the window and inside the courtyard, I heard at three o'clock or so a heavy *ting-ting-tinging* of rain and then came a serious shift in the sound and I knew that it was hailing. I dressed in a hurry and ran to the field. The unprotected grapes were being pummeled by hail, the baskets already covered with a layer of icy stones. I moved the baskets together and brought the donkey and wagon and began loading one basket after another, covering them from time to time. The hail was getting larger, and I knew I had to work fast to save the harvest. I moved the wagon to the shed, the donkey and I both pulling together. We got the first load in. By the second I was tired. By the third, although I was exhausted, I felt exhilarated. Then the wagon got stuck in mud and no pushing or pulling could get the wheel turning. I needed to lift it up and out. I put my shoulder to the axle and pushed, but it did not budge; again I tried, with all my strength I lifted. It did not move much, but I could feel a shift in the weight and I knew the balance was so equal between my strength pushing up and the weight of the wagon on my shoulder that if I let up for a second, the wagon would slip and turn over, causing havoc for the donkey and grapes and me. Then all of a sudden I felt my strength wane. You know that place? It is just between what you can do and what you can't. The place where you know that you might not go on. In a few minutes, I knew I could not support the weight, but just as the wagon was about to slip, "Help!" I said, and out of nowhere I felt Her step up beside me and then I felt Her put Her shoulder to the wagon and at the very spot that I was failing it moved up just enough to get the wheels turning and out of the ditch.

The donkey and I moved the last of the baskets into the closed sheds. Then, after following the donkey back, I went exhausted to my room and fell across the bed to sleep all day until night.

"Go out and away and enjoy yourself," the Uncle and Aunt said in unison. "We will take care of the house and ourselves as always, exactly as you young people expect," he added, looking at me slyly.

"Where is the Master Gardener?" I asked them.

"He's out tending his harvest and maybe sowing at this time."

"Perhaps I can help them."

"Them, them, him and them. Whom do you mean by 'them'?"

"I mean the Gardener and the people helping him."

"No, no, there are no people harvesting or planting with him, no help at all."

"In this you can't help him," Zia Graziella said.

Ziu Luiginu laughed out loud. "Help him do what? Find seeds that only a bird can see? Then go and shit it in the exact spot for spring?"

"Brother, it is one thing to take yourself to task and worry other donkeys about the place saying such things, but do not be so indelicate to a rosebud."

"Roses have thorns, Sister, and they had better get used to them if they want to go about making everyone faint with their fragrances. You are right about one thing, though. This rose will be able to open the eyes of anything with longing. I have noted it well."

"Fine, fine, but longing is how everything begins. Ah! Yesterday off the highest mountain terrace there was a great throw of crows tumbling and cawing in the air. You remember the day we watched them. The next morning we saw that they had planted the fields below, made everything

with longing and dancing. If not it would be winter forever, and we'd be tasting ashes. So many people think they are
practical, child, yet they do not see the *most* practical thing
under their noses. Cawing and tumbling is a mysterious
conjunctio, and all who try to explain cawing or tumbling as
separate events cause more trouble than their definitions
help clarify."

"NO DEFINITION IN SEPARATION," said the
Uncle in that seneschal's voice that I was getting used to.

"Yet we must wait, we must wait. I implore you not to
write it down yet. Spilled ink like spilled olive oil is bad
luck, and those invisible letters so many people write mes-
sages with are of no use at all, no matter how many people
use them. Besides, you never know how a story will turn,
go down with the mysterious clever plants or up in a tree
so you might have to erase this part and then worry about
where you can get more ink."

"True, we cannot write down the story yet, only tell it,
but I know today will end with cold and snow, and I'm
thinking we may have to commit this one to memory.
Besides, dear Sister, doesn't this story always end the same
way?"

"But this very day ends only as it will, and I guess that
it will end in cold weather as you predict. So then we'd better hurry to light the hearth in the old room. I have the
passionate songs ready. They are passionate so they are
sung with strong coffee," she added looking at me.

"You asked about planting and harvest. Maybe there
will be some time for us all to plant the little field of winter wheat, but that's not his affair, and to tell the truth,

Daughter, he does not like anything planted by humans."

"Because," added Zia respectfully, "he does not con-sider humans as good as the beasts for this kind of plant-ing."

"He definitely does not think so," they both said together, shaking their heads and heartily agreeing.

This is the way I kept up my lessons.

On a morning when nothing was happening, I started a proper journal, at first to continue to write down my "lessons" so that I could learn from them and then to record my new life faithfully. By accident I found the mar-gins of my empty school notebook useful for sketching furniture, objects, and places that were always showing themselves. At the time I still had an idea of reading some of this journal to my father and sisters so that they could understand my new life, but after a while I gave that idea up and became more interested in having no real "others" to write or paint for.

October 13

Today is the most beautiful of autumn days. I found a path which led to a walled garden of beautiful proportions filled with small plants and bushes heavy with fall berries. There is no end to "wild" gardens around the villa. But the land I see in the distance, but never reach, is desolate and barren without one large silhouette of a tree to be seen anywhere. This landscape, while dramatic and perhaps beautiful, is painful to see, as though the stones themselves are suffering.

October 15

After breakfast I found a room which has nothing in it but pots, the most beautiful, simple pots, ancient water jugs and pitchers. They are round and smooth with a strong black glaze, like something from a volcano, but they speak of work and use and beauty. Something about them demands felicity.

October 18

When I asked the Aunt about the pots, she said they were dug from the fields around the villa and are more than two thousand years old. There is a portfolio of etchings made of them in 1756. She said, "If you look carefully and listen they will be silent and you will learn about them." They are the simplest and most honest objects imaginable. I feel I have found a way to my own heart. Tomorrow I will look at them again and look for the portfolio. This quiet room is exciting.

October 19

Today when I went to see the pots, they were gone and instead the etchings of them were hung on the wall. I was surprised to see the pots gone and their likenesses left. At first I resented it, but after a long while I saw that the etchings were immensely satisfying for they taught the simple lesson of beauty in another way. I was amazed at this. The Uncle said, "Never put on the walls a painting of an object sitting next to it, a portrait next to the living person. It is bad manners and more!" The Aunt thought a while, then said, "It is a kind of shape change. But I am not sure what happens when you see them together. Must we think of this art as existing simultaneously or a little after the world or outside the world's time? I am not sure. Your pontification is interesting, Brother, but do we need to think of it as infallible?"

October 31, late in the afternoon

I saw the Master Gardener again today, walking thoughtfully through the rose garden. I went closer to see him but he left quickly. He wore no shoes.

The feasts of All Saints and All Souls passed. The nights were a little colder. The beautiful days of autumn were waning. And as the weeks of rain came in with days of storms, I started once again to stay around the house and explore its endless rooms. And like my father I found the room with the living plants of the ficus repens, the plants that had enchanted him. I had never been in a space which blended shelter with the outdoors, a quality the whole house shared. I sat there in the afternoons and did some awkward drawings. Once when looking up at a particular leaf I noticed a very slender stone door which I had mistaken for a crack in the wall. All doors and handles in this house invited curiosity, and I immediately turned the handle of the ring, and sure enough the door opened and I was in a closed courtyard with small carved pillars and on each there was a scene for which there seemed to be three sources: the Bible, classical mythology, and flowers, animals, and plants. My favorite pillars were devoted to the lives of insects and the teaching of the Blessed Mother by St. Ann. You know the one I mean, where the Virgin is shown as a child, with her mother, St. Ann, teaching her daughter lessons from the Bible. There is such sweet comfort and harmony in the close learning between figures and open book written in Hebrew. The cloister had a sweetness in all its proportions. In the center of it there was a garden, but it was not planted and at first I thought it was simply not cared for; then I saw that the piece of land was rich and each week, sometimes each day, another incredible bush or plant would be in bloom. The fragrance from this little bit of land was extremely pleasing. The hot, dry summers in this part of the country give a small herb a powerful aroma so the sage and salvia and rosemary all were fragrant. This little garden was so sheltered as to give the feeling that it was still summer here. A bush of edible laurel made a small hedge, and it was to this *Laurus*, Sweet Bay, that I came when I needed the herbal drink my grandmother used to calm stomachs and nerves called *acqua a lauru*. The cloister was my refuge in winter, and it was there that I saw the first blooming narcissus and wild cyclamen.

The days of winter were long. The Aunt and Uncle, shaping their lives to their own necessities, were not disposed to ordinary sleeping patterns. Once, in the middle of the night, I heard them reading aloud and went into the sitting room to find them reading poems from an old manuscript. They always read aloud, saying it was superior to "this new silent reading." "How can sounds reach your mind through your eyes only—the ears are needed!" proclaimed the Uncle more than once.

But since they were also up very early in the morning, moving around like mice putting things in their proper places, in the afternoons they were inclined to "shut their eyes a bit," "take a catnap," which sometimes lasted hours. During those catnaps, I got into the habit of going to the marvelous cloister, where I watched the life of plants change each day. So those little notations, which were at first marginal, now had pages to themselves, and I began to draw, learn to draw, that is. The cloister garden and mountain walks were the inspiration for these drawings.

Then one day, after showing the Uncle a clumsy attempt at a caterpillar on a shaky stalk, I came home to find on the dining table the marvelous album with insect metamorphoses (1683–1713), an album of original drawings by the great artist Maria Sibylla Merian, and beside it in even calligraphy was *For Rusina, so she can meet a master for her studies.* This artist had recorded flowers and plants and natural life, the most vivid of insects and their metamorphoses, painted on small watercolor paper glued to the right of a facing page in which she had noted in beautiful, even script the subject of the watercolor and her work with it. "This is the most artful nature book we have ever seen, Rusina," said the Uncle. From that day on, I studied it and the flora around the villa. Living with the book, I began to understand a kind of holy science that seemed so new and so ancient at the same time. "When curiosity is souled with beauty and respect, you have a *throw of crows,* so to speak," added the Aunt one day.

One evening, as I was dawdling at my place at the dining table, the door suddenly opened and the ugliest man I had ever seen walked quietly in the room and, bowing to me, sat down, but not before he presented me with a Book of Hours.

"This was my blessed mother's book. I thought you

might like to have it," he said, not looking at me but looking down at the table. His voice was deep and altogether beautiful, but his figure and face were so unusual that he almost did not look human. I hope that I did not shudder visibly. He said nothing after this, and my "Thank you" echoed in the room for a long time. He brought with him the quiet of beasts and also their sudden starting up. Without a word of warning, he rose from his chair and, bowing, said, "Good evening," and left without another sound.

This meeting excited me. He was so ugly that I do not even want to record it here, but I can tell you it was not the wide-set eyes or nose or his stooped figure or his great bearlike arms but altogether his demeanor. His gentle speech and beautiful voice rang in my ear long after he had gone; they were exquisite.

Having the Book of Hours, made centuries before, in my hands was like holding both history and eternity. The meditations were in a tongue that I could not read, but the illuminations were of the fauna and flora of the land surrounding the villa. I marveled at how familiar they were to me. And yet there were pages of illustrations of mountain lakes and surrounding forests, but they were nowhere to be seen. Had these once been real or were they fantasy?

For weeks I worked at improving my drawing, and I must say that I was not so good or so bad that Uncle didn't laugh and say, "Try again. It's close, but not too close, try again." And Aunt said, "Child, I can see you are going to get a diploma at the end of these studies. You are headed for at least one sheepskin I am sure." With all this encouragement, I continued error upon error, which always brought me close to what it was *I had not seen.* For as soon as my drawing was wrong, I would find some more to understand, and then when I had studied long enough Aunt would always say, "Let it live! Let it live!" Once, looking over a long series of wild thyme that was still blooming in the cloister, she said, "Did it tell you it was in such pain and wanted us to know? Or is that you longing? One is one and the other far from here, Child."

The Aunt was right for my sensibilities as well. And so I loved my days. And since there was a cold spell that winter, the Aunt and Uncle asked me to help them bring straw to a small house beyond the rose garden. I had no idea that it was there, and when we went I was amazed to see a small round house made all of hand-cut stones and sweet new straw to cover the stony ground and a deep fire pit in the center and above it the hole in the ceiling to let the smoke out. The walls were plastered inside and black from smoke. When we lit the fire it was quite warm. The night we arranged the ancient house it snowed. I had never seen snow in my life, and even here in the mountains it was infrequent said the Aunt.

"Misery of miseries, Sister, do you remember the first time we saw snow when we were children?"

"Of course I remember. Tell Rusina what happened."

"Well, it snowed and we children ran about eating the flakes with our tongues and covering ourselves in cold. We played and played and asked many questions. Then I got an idea. 'How can I save the snow so it won't disappear?' I asked my father. 'What can you do? Do you know anything that you can make that will last?' he asked seriously. I remember as if it were this morning. 'Pots,' I said, 'pots last.' 'Good! Make pots,' he told me, so I made pots out of snow all day and by evening, exhilarated and expectant, I had saved everything I could. 'Now,' said my father, 'you will have to bake them,' which, innocent that I was, I did. I trusted my father in everything. Well, you know what happened: I baked them and when I opened the oven they were gone . . . gone! I could not believe it. I cried."

"Betrayal is best, Brother. I have told you that again and again. Snow is snow, but betrayal is a great teacher and like baked snow it is eternal."

That night I went to supper exhausted and had thought so much of snow I had forgotten the Master Gardener.

"Good evening," he said. "Have you everything you need, Signurina Rusina?"

"Oh! More than I could ever desire . . . what may I call you?"

"My name is Sebastiano, and if you call me by my name I will feel happy," he said in a lugubrious voice.

"Fine! Signor Sebastiano, will you sit and have a coffee with me?"

He sat uncomfortably but took the cup I offered with such grace that if I hadn't had to look at his hand it would have been a pleasant enough exchange. We sat again in silence. Then he asked if I would play a song on the spinet, which I did, making at least two mistakes. But it all went well for he started to sing a song about a nightingale in autumn. When this was over, he rose and thanked me graciously and lumbered out, the coffee cup still in his hand.

The next day he did not come into the dining room, but he left a black enamel painter's box, filled with colors in bottles. Every one had its place, and my heart overflowed on touching each thing. The next day I worked from morning until night without a thought. By evening I was hungry and went into the dining room to see what had been left, and there he sat at the table. He rose and begged pardon and asked if he could sit with me at dinner. And so we ate together and he told me of two beautiful birds he had seen that day, a beautiful green waterbird fishing above a stream and a brown-and-red creeper that he had seen climbing the garden wall. I became determined to look at birds more closely. After that brief exchange, he waited until I put my knife and fork on my plate, and then he rose on that signal, bowed, and, without a word, left.

The next day a terrible wind blew, and the Aunt and Uncle sat on their sofas (he dragged his couch from his room) near the stove, and now I kept a good fire going for them and made them my bitter chicory soup.

"Not bitter, the potato makes it sweet. It's the only part I like, to tell the truth, Rusina; but I fear this is the kind of thing that is good for the stomach, and I don't know why I should do a good deed for my stomach since it is one of the major betrayers."

"You are full of logic tonight, Brother."

"Mostly potatoes and hot soup made by our dear Flower. I like to keep logic to a minimum, since it has never agreed with my liver, with which I try to be on good terms."

After that we all had a bit more wine, which was red and hearty and went well with my next dish, pulpettini and fresh beans. There seemed to be no need to comment on the rest of the meal, and we ate enjoying small talk about our neighbors in the village and news of the weather, which could be predicted, it seemed, by looking at the clouds each night which came marching over the mountains from the north.

D e c e m b e r ,
W h e n   T h o u g h t s   A r e   L o n g

This morning I could not leave my bed until I finished reading Christine's section on women painters. Although they are not usually mentioned in histories, I knew that women painted manuscript borders and miniatures. In the Book of Hours Sebastian left, in the border of a reading from Luke 10.38, there is a painter of miniatures in the dress of the day sitting at her easel painting a manuscript's flower border. It feels like a self-portrait. She is so absorbed that not even the droning of a wasp flying above her head disturbs her. I feel more like the wasp than like the painter today.

My paint box is both perfectly useful and beautiful. On the outside cover there is a painting of mountains and at the latch painstakingly written in even calligraphy the opening words of

The Metamorphoses—

> *"In nova fert animus mutatas dicere formas corpora"*
> *My mind inclines to talk of forms changed into new bodies*

> *—and on the inside is another scene with many different crea-*
> *tures drinking around a lake and above it is written*

> *To see things as they are is to drink from an endless cup*
> *—Anonymous*

The sky in winter had so many blues that I spent weeks just learning and experimenting with cobalt and cerulean. One day I went out of the villa hoping to find some new plant or bird when unexpectedly Sebastiano and I came upon each other. We were both surprised and had no ready words at first, but then he recovered and said, "I was searching for some flowers, but I seem to have misjudged the place. They are rare bulbs."

"Why is that?" I asked, and then I saw his brow change and color spread on his neck, and then he put his hand over his eyes and said in a steady quiet voice: "When I was a boy, I had a dream that I saw a great flat plain and it was filled with gently blowing wheat, and a tremendous variety of creatures lived there and among them was a small group of humans. But then I saw another plain where people were so plentiful and they began to grow in numbers and size so that soon I could not see the ground. A terrible roar came from overhead. At first I thought it was thunder but it never stopped as natural things do. The din was from a mechanical device which they had invented to carry them from one place to another. This noise never stopped, and there was nowhere to hide from this sound. Then just as night fell I looked around me and saw that there was not one field of grass, or plant, or tree anywhere. Since then I have been committed to the love of rare plants."

When he finished speaking, he was in such pain that I said nothing for a long while, and then I said a word of understanding and we parted courteously and awkwardly. He went back to his search and I went home thinking about his dream and how much of it had already come true. I was agitated by our meeting, and in my diary of that day I wrote, *Sebastian does his work with the greatest love and pain, and it is true that he does not admire the greater part of mankind or our inventions.*

It was at this time that I became interested in poetry, love poems in particular. I found the poems of Jacopo Da Lentini, the Sicilian poet the Aunt and Uncle read aloud. I now found his passionate love sonnets, written in 1233, exactly to my mind.

> *Amor e uno disio che ven da core*
> *per abondanza di gran piacimento;*
> *e li occhi in prima generan l'amore,*
> *e lo core li da nutricamento.*

> *Love is a yearning that comes from the heart*
> *from a flowing over of great beauty;*
> *and the eyes are the first to give it birth,*
> *and the heart gives itself for bread.*

Compared to my schoolmates, I had always been considered backward in this area of love. I was thought of as
attractive, maybe even "lovely," as our neighbors used to
say, but their sons' attentions never interested me. As far as
marriage was concerned I was suspicious. I had had very
little time to observe my parents' marriage, except to see
how sad my father was without my mother. By the time I
looked around, I found both men and women had insuffi-
cient reasons for going into that state which I saw as unim-
portant to me. After all, I did not want to forfeit the
absolute freedom that I hoped to gain one day. At that
young age, whenever I saw that love was often mixed with
survival or power rather than with freedom, I was secretly
glad to be uninterested in it. And yet I understood the line
lo core li da nutricamento (the heart gives itself for bread [sus-
tenance]). This giving of the heart seemed to be speaking
to me of my own life. If love did not interest me, why did
the heart speak so clearly to me? I loved no one, of that I
was sure.

"Do you know poetry, Aunt?"

"A little."

"Do you know any love poems?"

"I had a teacher once who read me Sappho."

"A teacher who sang to you in foreign tongues, Sister?
Didily tidily, do I know this grand person?"

"Oh, I think so, Brother. This teacher had a craggy
head, and when the wind whistled through the poplars you
could hear the strings of the old lute pluck lines that
would make my blood boil and I would go cavorting in
those fields like a lamb in spring and sing,

Come, Venus,
Come to me with your golden cup
Nectar blossoms float
Fill the goblet up
My giddy lips shall kiss the brim
And I will be devoted."

"The old poems will be remembered," he said.

"*As long as rivers flow and poplars bloom,*" they said together.

"Did you really feel so moved, Sister, that you cavorted? Did Mother know this? When exactly was this grand time?"

"Now, of course, like all time it is now. I still feel that way."

A   S a d   R e t u r n

My days and nights in winter were all alike, and there was not much work to do outdoors in fields or gardens, but the Uncle and I did put in the winter wheat and did go to the village each week to barter or buy or gossip, as the Aunt said. Twice some neighbors came, and there was music and stories and I loved that very much since it reminded me of my father. After meeting Sebastian on my walk, I did not see him for a week, until one day it snowed again, and that night at supper there was a knock on the dining room door and I knew that it was he.

"Do you permit me?" he asked.

"Yes," I said eagerly, wondering if he would tell me more dreams.

Then he came in and stood at the table. I motioned him to sit, studying him for a minute, and was reminded of my father's expression, *occhi di vicci*. It was true. Sebastian's eyes were small and black and as intense as the carob seed.

"I've come to bring you a message. A neighbor came to say your father is ill and wants you to go back home."

I became alarmed and knew that I would go to him at the first light. Sebastian took great pains to get me home as quickly as possible. But he was troubled at my leaving. At the carriage door, he helped me in and lingered before closing it. "Do you want to come back?" he asked.

I told him I would be back as soon as my father recovered. "I'm leaving you all my drawings and my painting box and next to it all my unfinished pages on the table. Please don't let anyone throw them out," I said, joking.

"Fine, fine," he said. "We wish your father a quick return to health and you to us again." He lifted my large case to the coachman, and off I went to travel back over the same road that had brought me.

But I had a bad feeling and said my prayers all the way home. It took a day, and then at night I was at our old door, which looked so different somehow, as though it wasn't the old door I knew, and yet it was, for there in front of me was the deep gash where Marta had thrown a candlestick at me. When I saw the old place I felt a pang of love and sorrow. My sisters greeted me at the door with their usual quick tears. "Finally, you came home,

Ungrateful One. You weren't here when Father needed you. Where did you get that outfit?" they asked. "And look at you! Look at you! What is happening there with those disgusting people?" And so on.

I went to my father and saw that he was near death. I was in a panic, and after days of trying everything we could, I saw he needed more than I could give. I sat beside him for three more days and nights, and we cried and held hands and remembered things together and prayed and said all our old jokes together and in the night between eleven and midnight his soul trembling on his lips left him. I was frozen with disbelief. The dumb pain that struck me then has never left me. I cannot tell you much of the funeral except to say everyone cried from all the villages around, and when it was over I went home and sat with my sisters "for just another week." They asked me what my life was like, and pretending to care, they used whatever I said to make fun of me in their old way. And once again, as though time did not exist, I slipped back into an old familiar custom that seemed inevitable. When I think of it now, I can't explain this forgetfulness, it was an absolute state of sleepwalking. Who was it who once again listened to their insults, cooked and cleaned and fetched? I even helped with preparations for the wedding of my older sister and gave them whatever it was of my clothes or jewels they desired. And so weeks passed and I stayed rooted to my old spot.

One afternoon, months after my father's funeral, while my sisters and I were sipping coffee, my old cat walked in and I picked her up and kissed her scrawny neck and I saw that she had gotten so thin that it pained me. As Marta poured herself another cup, Carmela jumped up from her seat and grabbing Miciu threw her down and by accident kicked Marta's chair, causing the coffee to spill down her front. "You stable shit," she hissed as Carmela smiled, putting a biscuit to her lips. And at that moment I put down my cup, picked up my Miciu, and walked out the door.

The *Ater* House and the Sooty Walls of Compassion

There was a heavy rain falling when I left my childhood home. In a short time, the coachman hitched the carriage to the harnessed horses and I drove away without another word to my sisters. The loss of my father was so great that even now, some years later, I cannot talk about it with equanimity; it was only the last loving words my father and I said to each other that gave me any comfort.

The ride home was difficult, rain and then mud on the roads. Cats cannot stay contained; even in their fear they want freedom, trusting their own wiles to ours, and I can't say they're wrong. Old Miciu and I had a hard ride in the

closed carriage; but by the time we arrived home we had
both forgotten any reason we had to be traveling anywhere,
and she ran in at the door and slipped under my bed and I
went in search of the Aunt and Uncle. The house seemed
cold, neglected. They were neither in the kitchen nor in
their sitting room. Neither the oven nor the hearth was lit.
They were not in any of their usual places. I looked for
them, all the time calling their names, but found no sign of
them and knew that there was not a usual explanation for
this silence. Had something terrible happened to them? In
a slowly growing fear I went to find Sebastian.

I wasn't sure where he slept, but I felt it must be the
old place that the Uncle and I had put in order. It was the
round house, made of large hand-cut stones, plastered on
the inside, the walls black with smoke, (*"Atrio, atrium, ater,*
black in Latin," I could hear the Uncle say), the small
interior for just one family, a fire pit in the center and
above it a hole in the roof to let out the smoke and let in
the light.

From a distance it too looked uninhabited, no smoke
or sound of any kind coming from it. I had a hard time
pushing open the door, which had roots stuck under it. The
place was unwholesomely damp and so dark I could not
easily see. It looked as though it had been dug up from
beneath, two mounds of dirt and a pile of roots and
tubers. It was filled with the acrid smell of a cold fire pit
and the unusually sharp smell of something I could not
identify. All the earthy contents of the room were in con-
trast to the light coming from above. This single beam of
light coming from the roof was like a benediction and gave

the room an unusual calm. I followed it to where it illuminated one more heap of earth and roots and leaves thrown in the corner. I was just about to turn and leave the place when my mind's eye remembered something and I turned, bent down, and put my hand on that dank mound and found the curled, hunched body of Sebastian. He was not moving and my first thought was that he was already dead. But when I touched his chest I saw a slight, intermittent breathing. I called his name, he did not stir, and I called again, then sat down next to him and took his cold hand. At this touch I could feel all his life move to his hand, as though he knew I was there. A great feeling of sorrow and pity came over me.

I ran to the villa and got the wheelbarrow, where I put quilts, pots, water, food, and anything else I could think of that might help Sebastian. After covering him, I built a small fire in the pit with the windfalls I had picked up and a good blaze quickly started. Soon the small room was warm and dry. For the next hours I felt his life shake and I doubled my efforts. I cradled his heavy head and a shudder ran through me. His hair and beard were so damp and unkempt as to feel, look, and smell like something dying at the edge of the sea. A shudder ran through me again and he moved. I touched his dry lips with water from my dripping hand and he stirred.

"Sebastian, are you awake? Can you drink this cup of tea?"

"Yes, yes," he rasped, and I gave him a warm drink of sweet and pungent herbs until he closed his lips, his heavy head sinking back again. Outside the strong wind moved and it began to snow, occasional flakes swirling down to melt in the warmth of the black *ater* room.

For three days and nights, as the blizzard heaped snow against the door, we stayed in that old room. Only once I went back to the villa to gather more food and herbs and carry Miciu. Not caring if it was day or night, I cooked and slept and cared for Sebastian. There were moments I thought he had recovered and then soon afterward there would be a falling back and I saw him near death. In the end it felt like the grace of God when he opened his eyes. "You are back. I thought I was having a beautiful dream," he said, moving himself to the water and bending over it to drink delicately. After a very long drink he looked up at me and thanked me with few words.

"And the Aunt and Uncle?" I asked.

"They've gone to Palermo," he said as he fell back on his bed, sighed deeply, and slept untroubled for many hours.

On the morning of the fourth day, when the snow and wind had stopped, I pushed open the door with all my might and let in the cold and brilliant sun. Sebastian was not completely recovered. For the next two days I returned to make the *ater* house as comfortable for him as I could, bringing food that I cooked at the villa. The snow was now almost completely gone, and the sun left almost nothing of the blizzard except for the fallen trees and an overall disarray in the land. That first day I saw many small animals and birds who had survived come out with an urgency that made them vulnerable to hunters. Included in this was a flock of lapwings which I took the time to draw for my

"Accounts Book," which was what I now called my nature diary. I brought my paper and paint box back with me into the *ater* house, where I drew the roots and leaves and plants and debris which I saw. When my eyes grew accustomed to the light, I made out a pile of bulbs whose hairy roots and shapes I would not have thought good subject matter for drawing, but as I watched the light and dark show their prodigious diversity, I saw that they were beautiful.

"I see you like roots and bulbs," he said, looking at the drawings. Then looking closer he showed me what he saw in them. He talked about bulbs of hyacinths and crocuses and lilies—"Buds under the earth," he said—and brought fields of flowers to my imagination.

"I hope you like my cat," I said, moving through some quick sketches I had made of Miciu and Sebastian sleeping.

"How can I not like Miciu, who helped to save my life?" he responded. It was true that at times Miciu had slept in the crook of his legs.

That evening I brought him some soup and two new drawings. I put both down and was surprised to see that Sebastian was sitting up in his bed sewing. At first I didn't believe my eyes, for he was sewing my old jacket. "I hope you don't mind," he said. "I saw that it was torn."

"No, I don't mind," I said. "It is very generous of you, and I see by your work that you are quite well again and that you know how to make fine small stitches." I found there was no end of surprises in him.

By the end of the sixth day Miciu and I were back home, and soon after that the Aunt and Uncle returned as well with many stories to tell. I told them of the death of my father and they were pained for me. They understood very well and that helped me in my sorrow. I told them about Sebastian's illness and suggested we visit him. "Oh, he won't be at the old house now. I'll bet you," said the Uncle.

"No bet," said the Aunt. "You can never tell where wild-flowers will turn up, not like planting a field of fava beans!"

Sebastian came to join me for dinner that night. He still looked grisly, but I had the grace of not mentioning it to him. He asked to see the drawings and watercolors of the bulbs and the lapwings. "I will show you plants grow-ing in hidden places," he said. All the while he spoke of flowers, I saw that his mind was preoccupied. Then finally when he was leaving he sat down again and asked abrupt-ly, "Will you marry me, Rusina?"

I could not speak for a long while, which is death to all urgent requests of love. Finally I said, "Sebastian, I like you very much as a friend, but for a husband I must say no."

At the time I would have said, "Please, let nothing more change."

For Days They Sang and
Spoke Only of Music

When the discussions of music and Palermo subsided, the Aunt added, "You should have seen the beautiful hand-carved balconies at the opera house!"

"Balconies? How can you talk of balconies when we heard divine music matched by divine singing and crying?!"

"Yes, balconies. We were closer to them than to the singers. Where we sat I saw every exquisite leaf and figure. They are beautifully designed, beautifully carved. You know, Rusina, it cost the master builder more to finish them than the municipality paid him."

"Now how do you know that, Sister?"

"Because, Brother, our cousin Angelina's husband, Alfonso, is the master builder who designed them, and it was her money that paid for making them. Instead of two years to complete they took four. Master builders! They are deliciously uninterested in time and money like the best artists. Alfonso is the most heartfelt man in the world. The two of them respect and love each other very much. Of course, the hard part was that they had to be away from the village for so long, but then Angelina loves when stories are knotted and then unknotted. In this story she was able to do the unknotting."

"You never cease to amaze and surprise me, Sister."

"The music, Rusina, amazed and surprised as well," she said, turning her face with a little cat smile.

"Talking of money is never pleasant, so very indelicate. Forgive us, Rusina. But we have something to give you— the money we owe you for your work."

"Oh, no," I said. "Please, it should be reversed. It was Sebastian who was owed money for the ship."

"No, dear girl, this is money for your work and independence. Unless they are in a place where talent, heart, and intelligence (both practical and theoretical!) are measures of strength and authority, women need money to keep themselves in this new world. But where is that place?

No, no, believe me at this time, there is nothing to replace having your own money if you also want independence. Talent and ability are like oil sliding down a funnel into a leaky jar, and these money fools measure even their own value only by money."

"We have all learned that the barter system is over. Trust us, every woman needs her own money," said Ziu Luiginu. "It doesn't have to be a great deal—just enough for roof and bread to live as one chooses. And you, my dear, have earned that."

"And here it is," they both said together, the Aunt handing me the packet and the Uncle saying, "We know there are those that get a bit of money all at once and squander it because they put it in place of character. Oh, Child, if we thought that, we would burn this right now. Oh, no, you have plenty of strong character!"

"Because of this, you will not have to suffer fools gladly," said the Aunt, laughing uproariously. "Tell me, Brother, what did you mean by saying we heard divine singing and crying at the opera?"

"Which, the 'singing' or the 'crying'?"

"'Singing,' of course; we all know about 'divine crying.'"

There was no stopping them; and after the bit of understandable sense, they began to make their usual sense again, and I haven't the composure to record it I am still so moved by their generosity.

I put this money away and, since I did not have much need for it, forgot it for a while. It was like the dresses and books I had found in my first days here, only now it was the packet of money that was tied with lovely red silk thread with my name on it.

That winter was a time of extremes. After the storm there was a warm winter week and after that a week of chill and rain. We moved into a life of deep memory and musings. Days at the fire, the Aunt told about their childhood, and the Uncle sang his favorite songs, childhood ditties that we sang with him. One day Sebastian, who had come to bring us cabbage for dinner, came in and sat in the corner and watched us with pleasure. We convinced him to stay and eat dinner with us. Afterward the Aunt said, as though speaking important words to a favorite acolyte, "Signurina Rusidda, would you go to the pantry and get us the ricotta and sugar?" Everyone waited until she mixed the right combination and a beautiful pudding was put into small plates and eaten with tiny spoons. The Aunt has the knack of making feasts with hardly anything.

The storytelling evenings were the most eventful during that month of cold. One night the neighbors came to hear the Aunt tell the old stories. Entire families came—all the children and even babies in arms, men with caps in hand, and women in their best shawls. All evening long the Aunt told the old stories, and it was a great comfort and pleasure shared by all of us. She sat like an empress; her long skirt covered the charcoal brazier that warmed her very cold toes. She warmed us all that night with her stories, and we would not let her go.

I remember one story about an old woman and the month of March.

"Of course, writing it down is not telling it. You must

tell it," said the Uncle when he repeated the story so I could write it in my journal. "There is feeling in the gestures and in the voice, and much is told by the silences and whispers, by the suggestions and the secrets shared with the listeners, who when the story is ended can feel that they knew the significance already, knew it in their bones, knew it like meeting yourself in a mirror—it might take you by surprise but there is no doubt who it is."

It is told and retold (*Si cunta e si raccunta*) that once the last day in the month of March was warm and springlike so a very old woman rejoiced and taking off her heavy winter shawl set out on a long walk. "I have survived another winter and I've beaten you, you old March dog!" she said spitting.

But her daughter saw this and said to her, "Don't go on a long walk, Mother, and don't leave your shawl behind; you never know what the end of the day might bring." But the old woman would not listen and off she went. March heard her, became very angry, and went to his sister April to ask her if he could borrow one of her days. Of course, his sister obliged him.

On the first day of April, the daughter said, "Don't give up your warm clothes, Mother, and don't leave the house." But she did not listen and by the afternoon when she was far from home it began to snow. It snowed and snowed for two days. Caught by the storm, the old woman arrived home ill and spent all of April in bed and was lucky to survive it at all.

And they lived happy and content and here we are looking for our good work.

"So much for calling March a bad name," said the

Uncle the next day, making a secret sign against any retribution March might visit on him.

"Wearing that heavy shawl might have helped. You'd think she had lived long enough to know better," I said without much poetry or thought. I still measured every death with my father's.

"It would have made little difference," said the Aunt.

"I think it's a story for young people really. It shows them how to behave to the old."

"But you notice how stubborn old age is," said the Uncle. "The daughter does her best but the old one is also the Old One, Winter itself, and Winter cannot win the battle with Spring."

". . . any more than we can win it with death."

"The old woman simply did not use her common sense. Winter was not over and especially not at the end of March. She should have known enough to wear her shawl and that is that."

"I'm surprised, Brother, you don't say it's a story spun by the shawl merchants just to sell shawls."

"Oh! I just might add that to my list the next time. I'm sure there are those who would believe it."

"The stories are simple but not so simple," I said.

"True. Be suspicious of those who tell you this is naïve. It is as naïve as finding a snake in the bread box," said the Aunt.

"It is true," said the Uncle. "These old stories are like the parables, they tell us what we know but have strangely forgotten, until we hear it again and we say, 'Oh! Yes. Of course.'"

The storytelling continued for the next weeks. Everyone came filing into the sitting room and hours passed together. Gossip and jokes with little drinks and biscuits when it was ended.

During the days Miciu and I loved the cloister. We sat in the sun in that protected space when the world was cold. We smelled narcissus and all kinds of delicate flowers until we were dizzy with pleasure. And then one day I saw the rosebush blooming, the one with a red as dark as blood, the one that rested so completely I thought it must be dead, and there that morning the first thin and delicately pointed leaves were showing. My first watercolors of the new blooms were hopeless, but I continued and in the end Sebastian could name what I had drawn.

He came each evening. We talked so easily and well together, spent our time in the evenings like friends, but I must add that although I felt full sympathy for him he was not in any way attractive to me. His face and form were so strange that at times he was slow and deliberate and at other times he had the look of a fox, nervous to be else-where, and I always avoided touching him even when passing a spoon.

On a Friday night in late January, after a beautiful sunny day hinting at spring, Sebastian came after dinner. He lingered longer than usual and then with his head slightly bowed said, "Will you marry me, Rusina?"

It took a minute to compose myself and a minute for politeness before I was able to say, "I can't marry you. I love you as a friend, Sebastiano, but not as a husband."

And with that he bowed again and left. The following

Friday he asked again, and again I felt a tremor and again refused him. "You are too ugly" (*si troppo laidu*), I wanted to say but did not. But that would have been the truthful reason that I could not even imagine marrying Sebastian. And yet I knew that he had been generous with me and all my family and that his generosity was from some never-ending bounty I had seen in my own father's love.

This question of beauty or Beauty troubled me. How could love be so connected to attraction and beauty? I was so sure of my own moral and idealistic stance about the world that when I saw my own abhorrence to Sebastian's brutish ugliness I was ashamed. This abhorrence I can say was almost instinctive. Jacopo says love is a yearning which comes from the heart, which comes from *piacimento,* which in our medieval language means beauty. But Jacopo was not a foolish man. What kind of beauty was he talking about? The Aunt said that God needed us for real transformation, and I knew that this somehow had to do with the question of Beauty, but I could not connect them in my heart.

February 4

Today I have been studying my teacher's book and am amazed at her consistent intelligence and ability. The beauty of the watercolors is so moving that I cannot believe the sensual joy contained in the calm surface. Maria Sibylla Merian as a child watched silkworms in her mother's garden and was so excited by the metamorphosis that years later she went to the West Indies to learn from the insects there. The album is felicitous and beautiful. I wish I could meet and talk with her and find out more about her techniques. They are beyond my ability. I need the intense seeing and knowledge which Sebastian's visits inspire in me. It is not that he

loves drawing but that he loves what I draw and sees in it the pos-
sibility of spirit beyond or inside the lines and colors so that his
comments come from a depth which my drawings must match. He
is truly a Master Gardener. He knows about the thing he loves so
completely that he makes no ignorant gesture toward it. But when
he talks to me I still avert my eyes; I cannot stand to look at him,
and I wonder at my feelings for him. Why am I so unfair? Why
does his form so affect me? Can't there be some forgiveness for
nature's way or for my own limited sense of beauty? Is it that I
am not seeing the spirit inside the lines and colors? Am I not being
faithful to the original so that I cannot love what comes with the
spirit? What journey must I make to see that?

But since love is not rational no amount of reasoning
furthers Sebastian's courting.

February 20

Today the scent of lemon blossoms was in the air. I found a small
tree in the corner of the cloister beginning to bloom. I seem to have
an affinity for these; the watercolors were spontaneously "right."
The green of the leaves took me time. It is warm in the garden.
My notebook is getting fat.

I have been studying a page from Elizabeth Blackwell's botan-
ical prints that she hand-colored. A page of fava beans. The Uncle
and I love this drawing. It is so simple and correct and soulful.
"Let's plant fava beans, Rusidda."

The End of Winter

There are either pages missing from my journal or nothing of note happened or so much of note happened I
couldn't bear to record it. I do remember that at this time
Miciu and I spent entire mornings in the cloister. And in
the afternoons the Aunt and Uncle and I measured roads
and alongside them stands of trees so that they would not
be cut down for the wide carriages which were the rage.
Aside from measuring and taking notes for the authorities
we spent most of the time seeing frescoes in remote
churches.

We all got our throats blessed on February third for St.
Blase, even the Uncle, who was critical of anything
"Official" like governments and religions and official posi-
tions that he considered never sensible. "And that priest,"

he said, "I can't stand to hear his unctuous pretending voice, as though he can hide anything from us. We'd have to be really stupid to believe that kind of lying piety. Why can't he just speak plainly as his Teacher spoke?"

"I believe St. Blase has helped your throat, Brother, but I don't know what saint to appeal to when one is under the siege of haranguing."

"Nicely put, Sister, and well taken. I will put this stone down and be quiet."

We had a wonderful time going around "getting holy by looking at art and loving the Master Teacher and His Beautiful Mother," said the Aunt. These journeys allowed us to try the neighboring restaurants—often homey affairs where the lady of the house brought out a selection of more or less fresh food and asked us which we wanted and then gave us the choice of how we wanted it cooked. Mostly we were satisfied and always grateful since these pilgrimages made us especially hungry as well as particularly unruly.

Before Lent

Then well before Lent, with a bare hint of spring, people dropped in to talk about the ball that is always given on the Tuesday night just before Ash Wednesday. Everyone in town is invited to the villa for carnival, and it is a costume ball with dancing and prizes and a champagne punch bowl "which the men will mostly ignore, drinking their own wine that they carry up from the valley. There are many surprises hiding in corners," the Aunt told me. "Don't miss this dance, young lady. Gowns and uniforms, animals and bishops, ladies and gentlemen, Cyclopes and courtiers—all will be there."

"What should I wear?" I asked the Aunt.

"I don't know. Fool us! But whatever you do you must dance. The young men will ask you to dance. Definitely it is a time to think of exciting things. Have you been reading love poetry?"

"Lately, I haven't thought much about love, Zia."

"It's a powerful thing. It seems to live its own life, this love. Be careful, dear; if you think March gets offended easily, it is nothing compared to Love. It is a great mystery, and catching hold of it by the tail does not help. You end up with nothing for your troubles but a bite. Remember, costumes are needed for the ball."

I could not think of any until I saw the set of colored prints in my room of personifications of Love and Poetry and Trust, dark-eyed women as flowers. I enjoyed the thought but never took out the scissors and needle.

There is some concern about Sebastian. No one has seen him for days.

It is not full spring but the days are filled with sun and everywhere flowers have come up suddenly and abundantly. I cannot wait until May for I know then that the entire Island will be in bloom, the fragrance so sweet that one smiles all the time, heady with divine flowers. The roses beginning their long season, sweet jasmine growing with climbing roses, all the trees blooming, then here in the center fields and mountain meadows are carpets of pink and red and purple clover, convolvulus, irises, violets, and sweet narcissus. It is no accident that the story of Ceres and Proserpina happened here on the lands around the villa.

It will all happen in time, now that we are all outdoors planning a larger kitchen garden. "Working hard, praying, hoping, and gambling—that's what farmers do," said the Aunt. "Look at your uncle over there. He has his heart set on that wheat and on that beanfield. Let's wish him luck," she said and struck the earth. Sebastian is back, and when I met him on a walk in the mountains I knew how much I had missed him. He showed me two secret places where rare flowers grew. I must come tomorrow with my paint box and try to record them before they are gone. He was courteous, as always, and I did not ask him where he'd gone. As usual he looks away when I talk to him. His eyes are so terrible that I think if I were a child I would run from him. They are either absent, innocent, or piercing. His clothes are worse than ever and his appearance so unkempt. Yet when he speaks of flowers and walks in the field I am amazed by him. He is altogether the kindest man I have ever met. My grandmother would have called him "truly noble." I thanked him for the secret places and said goodbye, leaving him at the old dark house.

I have been making portraits of spiders. I love them and can watch them for a long time, a long time. I'm beginning to recognize the individuals and there is one jumping spider that I swear I would know anywhere.

Tonight at dinner there was a great excitement. We talked of "living scenes" that are being created for the ball. The Uncle, I imagine out of his familiarity with snow, is making a tableau straight out of a picture book of Russian winter scenes. The Aunt said, "It will be an elaborate sled with intricate decorations on all

sides. A sled with proper blades—everyone who works on it with
him marvels at his imagination, especially since they themselves
have never seen such a thing before." Every year he asks two friends
to sit in his sled in overcoats and heavy fur scarves; then another
friend, wearing a Russian skating outfit (with skates in her hand),
stands at the sled about to be helped in. They even make confetti
for snow. It is a tableau among four others presented each year at
the ball. This one is always the same but the others change and are
always a surprise. "He is fixated on snow," said the Aunt.
"Someday he will cause a fantastic and marvelous blizzard."

"Come to the shed, Rusina, and see what I am making for
the scene this year."

"Go, Rusina," the Aunt said. "Expect much. Imagination is
all."

But I am getting worried. I have nothing special for the ball.
The Uncle said, "Draw yourself a costume of something that
truly interests you and we'll help you make it." The only thing that
interests me these days are the spiders. Too bad I can't imagine
what kind of costume I might make. Perhaps this is an affair I
will watch from outside or go in a simple dress but put a mask
on. That might be enough. Yes, I will make a spider mask and that
will be my costume.

Tonight Sebastian came to dinner and brought me a present. It
was a fancy ball dress with embroidery of insects and roses. It is
amazing. The roses have thorns and the insects are in all stages of
their lives. It is quite accurate and unsentimental. There is even a
tiny diaphanous spider weaving a web. Now I will put my efforts
into the mask. He tells me that everyone in our village and the
neighboring ones will be there.

"And will you be there, Sebastian?"

"Yes, I hope to be there."

"Do you dance?"

"Yes, I do. Will you dance with me, Rusidda?"

And without thinking I said, "Yes, I will dance with you."

"Then I will think of nothing else until the dance."

"My dancing, Sebastiano, is not so experienced."

"Then we will dance discreetly among the revelers and be unnoticed, except to each other."

It interests me how he can barely speak at times, and yet when it comes to love he has a nimble and appropriate tongue. If love does that I am pleased, if it's experience I am amazed.

I made my mask and it was not a spider after all, but a simple black mask with roses climbing in and out of my hair and brow as though my entire head was a wild rose tree. It pleased me and when I looked into the mirror I was surprised: I did not look like myself and that made me feel wonderfully strange, playing a rose.

"My Mind Inclines toward Transformations"

The day of the ball had come; it was being held in a huge crystal room, a high glass-domed plant house that was no longer used. The vignettes were arranged along the walk and I passed scenes that could have been dreams: a dance in an eighteenth-century palace drawing room; a mythological scene of Diana after the chase; the Uncle's Russian winter scene, sled bells and all; and a scene of the Pharaoh's daughter finding the baby Moses in the bullrushes. Lanterns lit the paths and the men and women were coming on foot, in carriages, on horseback and don-keys. The place was a proper carnival. When I entered the ballroom, it looked like a palace which had magically sprung up overnight, lit with thousands of candles burn-ing in all kinds of elaborate candelabras: it was outrageous beauty. The illumination in the room made everything into light and deep shadow; the dancers with their masks and costumes were unreal. The villagers and the inhabitants from other villas and farms in the neighborhood had all turned out and their outfits were ancient and imaginative. Some wore their grandparents' clothes, some had made outfits to resemble animals and birds, and there were the usual devils and angels, cupids and pirates. Everyone was masked, and it truly was impossible to recognize a familiar form. I went about thinking I could find the Aunt and Uncle but could not. And where was Sebastian? I felt I would have no difficulty seeing him, but he too was nowhere to be found. The room was already crowded. My dress was just right. It fit me perfectly and my rose mask went well with it. So in the end I did look like one of the paintings of personified flowers (the Rose as Poetry) except that my mask gave me no human face and I looked more strange and "other" than I had imagined.

At the ball the colors and shapes were so varied and pleasing that I enjoyed the first hour just walking about and looking at everything and everyone. The tables were heaped with food and cornucopias unbelievable to imag-ine. From where had such richness come? The music began immediately at nine, and the masked players reeled off folk dances as well as minuets and gavottes. This was my first ball. I was sitting in a chair in a corner of the room watching the dancers whirl around when I became aware that a door to the left had opened and in walked a man with a mask that had shining eyes made of shell. These beautiful and luminous eyes shone in the darkness and I was attracted to them and him immediately. He walked over to me and in a soft and full voice asked, "And, so, will you dance with me?" He offered me his hand. I took it and off we went. It was a traditional village dance and we joined three other couples for a good long while. The two of us danced well. And I was grateful when once or twice he caught me up from a mistake and saved our rhythm. When the music began again, we and our comrades all agreed to dance another set just as we were. And that went perfectly. His gloved hands gathered me and let me go, and I in turn turned with easy abandon, touched his fine waist, went round and round and then let him go. Our feet and hands and bodies danced heartily in a way I had never known before. When the music stopped, we sat down together and immediately a ferret came up to us with glasses of champagne punch which my dancing partner took off the tippled tray and, caressing my hand open, offered me a cup. And then a second cup as we sat out another dance. The next dance was a minuet, and he was up to it with pointing toes and delicate hands and wrists, more agile and lissome than any other dancer.

In harmony with the spirit of the ball, we did not tell our names to each other, but when the music began I thought I heard my name whispered as he rose and offered his hand, which I gladly took as off we danced to a tarantella. And then another and then another and finally we both said aloud and at the same time, "Stop!"

I thought *a moment of reprieve* and he must have been thinking the same thing for when I walked straight out the door he followed me. I led him to a rose garden which was enclosed and warm and smelled so peppery that we both breathed in the fragrance deeply before sitting on a bench together. There was a tinkling sound of water from a corner fountain. We sat for a while not saying a word and I took off my rose mask and put it carefully at my side. He had taken off his gloves and sat with his handsome legs spread out abandoned before him as young men sit, lethargic one minute but ready to spring up the next. He was so pleasing that I missed touching him, and when he linked his arm in mine, after an exquisite pause I took my hand and slowly opened his closed fingers one by beautifully one so that I entwined his fingers gently in my own. I looked up at his face and his shell-eyed mask shone in the darkness like the moon and I looked away—it was too bright—and when I looked back he was unmasked, and sitting there beside me was the most beautiful being I had ever seen. He took my breath away. His face was so perfect in its proportions. He had smooth cheeks and curly black hair. His violet eyes were soft and engaging, and there was no mistaking his slightly opened lips. He bent his head toward mine and we kissed. I felt so transformed that I had, in an instant, slipped my own skin and now had to wait until this new being was ready. We sat for a long time after this embrace. Then holding hands we walked about the garden before we slipped on our masks and went back to the ball. As we left the garden there was a strong scent of almond blossoms in the air.

At the ball we danced and danced, but did not speak a word to each other or embrace again. When the ball was over he pressed my hand to his heart and whispered in my ear, "And will you marry me?" I was surprised. We walked back to the villa with a crowd of young people and quietly took leave of each other. The boisterous crowd left laughing and merry, and I slipped quietly back into my room and changed my clothes. I could not sleep and I walked about touching things as though they were not there. I went into the kitchen but there was no light, the stove cold. Aunt was not in her room, and although I could not find anyone, the house itself was filled with consequence. At the atrium pool a feeling overwhelmed me, and I knew that I missed Sebastian. A red moon was shining down as large and close as I have ever seen, and without a lantern I went out to the *ater* house to see if there was smoke coming from the chimney, but there was none.

When I returned I heard a comforting snoring coming from the bedrooms and even Miciu had returned. The ball had been thrilling and I spent the sleepless night remembering and forgetting.

———————

"My Beast, My Beast, I Want My Beast"

The next morning, the Aunt, wearing every dress she owned or dreamt of, sat on her couch writing near the lit stove, looking more fabulous than most did the night before. This caused the Uncle and me to say together, "Are you still at the ball?"

"Are you still in costume, Sister?"

"Please find me some powders, dears, or at least a new good word for a headache."

"Too much champagne?"

"Not enough, Brother. Did you have a lovely ball, Rusina? I saw you only once and you were dancing with a man who looked like the Man in the Moon—quite beautiful!"

"I don't know the man's name, but he was a perfect dancing partner and very handsome."

"The monkeys are handsome too, dear."

"Remember the ones that were put onto trains in China so that they would not get caught by the first snows and die?"

"Oh, yes! But do they still have that sort of train service? I would have liked to avail myself of it this past winter. It was too cold."

"Well, we may be waiting a long time for anyone to bring that train, no drivers or conductors will give their time to it."

"True, true, Brother, awfully true."

Then they both fell silent. "Nice sound this room has," said Uncle. We sat waiting, receptive as toads. What peace!

Finally, the Aunt whispered, "He has come. Oh, blessed day that brings me sweet bread and water which I can taste." And she took out from the pile that was herself the "poems I am working on" and "poems I am waiting for." She called them "tattered musings." The Uncle and I left her sitting there by the old stove writing and waiting. I marveled at her new energy.

"Better, Rusina, than money or anything in hand is this Muse that is speaking to your aunt. Anyway," the Uncle said, shaking his head and laughing, "for the likes of us, for the likes of us."

They were back in form and I was listless. I went for walks with Miciu all day. At supper Sebastian did not come. I had a bowl of soup and read some pages from my Book of Hours, feeling the sore need of older faith and familiar comfort. *There are many gifts and one spirit.*

That night I had a dream that geese had called me out to follow them to a new place where I could travel over mountains and up and down the stairs of an ancient city to experience my new and old lives simultaneously. The next night and the next I spent in agitation, and finally on the third morning in the cloister I began to do watercolors, only now I painted the ball and the face of the stranger who haunted me into drawing him masked and unmasked. When I had filled a book and had gotten no closer to his beauty, wild cyclamen came to me and in some frenzied minutes I did a series of quick drawings of their butterfly flowers perched exactly right. They must have been individuals I knew by heart.

Later in the morning I went into the kitchen, where there was a great discussion going on. The Aunt and Uncle passed a letter back and forth as though they did not want to touch it until finally the letter was passed to me. I held it and the game stopped. Then the Uncle said, "It's for you, Rose." "What is it? Who is it from?"

I knew who it must be. "Do you know who this is?" I asked. They both shrugged and shook their heads no. I sat down and read a love letter from my beautiful dancer asking me to marry him. When I read this my feelings became clear and I said aloud with great certainty, "But who knows him?"

Then like a marionette scene the kitchen suddenly became alive, and everyone began to work: the Uncle putting away the drawings of his sled scene with grander plans for next year, the Aunt still jotting down the poems she now read us between a frenzy of soup making, and I cleaning and setting straight the whole room. By late afternoon there was calm again and I sat at the kitchen table drawing bowls and pots. "I didn't know we had so many beautiful pots," I said aloud.

"And some of them without lids," added Uncle Luiginu. Our life was being baked as bread.

Later that evening I was sitting in the dining room when there was a knock at the door, then the Uncle's footsteps, then the door opening, and in the distance I heard familiar voices.

I sat for a long time until finally with my "Accounts Book" in hand I got up from the table and there standing in the doorway was Sebastian. Everything felt familiar. I held my hand out to him, and when he put his hand in mine I smiled and a great warmth came over me and I drew him into the room.

"And will you dance with me, Rusina?"

"I would love to dance with you, Sebastian."

He smiled and began to hum and then sing an old tune in his soft clear voice. We danced to this music with feeling. And I noticed that he was dressed as a village bridegroom and he was pleasing to me.

"And will you go with me every May to find the wild orchids in bloom?"

"Yes."

"And may I sit quietly while you record the secret beauty they have shown you?"

"Yes," I said taking his hand.

"And will you marry me, *Bedda Rusina?*" And I kissed his lovely lips and then said yes to Sebastian, my muse, my friend, and my lover.

"And, Sebastian, will we live together here?" and he answered with a triumphant sigh, "Yes, *Bedda,* yes."

And then something small, almost imperceptible changed in the spirit of the room, a small opening, and there before me was a transformation, a grace given. Sebastian filled always with spirit now changed in form to me, and this man, this Master Gardener, was looking at me with his beautiful soft eyes with as much love as I have ever seen. And I knew him and he was as beautiful to me as my own life.

In Illo Tempore

The next day when they were talking he said, "My favorite part of the story, Rusina, is when you take my hand and look into my eyes and see me."

"As always, mine, Sebastian, is now when you will say for the first time and again: 'This has happened not because we have loved beauty but because it has loved us.'"